DEADGIRL

A NOVEL BY
BRIDGETT NELSON

BASED ON THE SCREENPLAY BY
TRENT HAAGA

Encyclopocalypse Publications
www.encyclopocalypse.com

Deadgirl: The Novelization
Based on the screenplay by Trent Haaga

ISBN: 978-1-966037-10-1

Cover Design and Formatting by Sean Duregger
Original Poster Artwork by Gadi Harel, used by permission
Interior design and formatting by Sean Duregger
Edited by Christine Morgan

FOREWORD

"RICKEY"

SHILOH FERNANDEZ

Eighteen years ago, I was driving down Wilshire Boulevard, clutching a stack of MapQuest directions and preparing for an audition that would change my life. I was young, green, and had little clue as to what I was doing. But something about this one felt right. It was dark and strange and unique. It felt like some force beyond my control or understanding was drawing me toward…*Deadgirl*.

Initially, I was asked to audition for JT. I'd been memorizing his lines for days. But as I drove east through Los Angeles, trying to make sense of the printed directions, a nagging thought took root: I wasn't JT. I was Rickie. His character resonated deeply with me; I could see my own struggles with loyalty, morality, and identity reflected in his journey. Yet, the idea of asking to read for a different role seemed risky, especially since I was still learning how auditions worked.

When I arrived, Matthew Lessall, the casting director, was kind enough to humor my request and offered me sides for Rickie. Nervous, but inspired, I took a moment before walking into the room. As the camera rolled, I spoke about my connection to Rickie and why I believed I was right for the part. My audition wasn't fantastic, but they saw something in my empathy toward this flawed character. Somehow, I got the role.

Written by the absurdly talented Trent Haaga, *Deadgirl* wasn't afraid to dive into the darkest corners of human nature, exploring themes like toxic masculinity, the objectification of women, and the ethical boundaries of desire. The script spoke to me in ways few had, serving as a true cautionary tale for young men of any generation.

Only a few years prior, I was in high school dealing with rejection, stepdad issues, and a yearning for self-understanding, which is one of the many reasons *Deadgirl's* rawness and complexity stood out from other 'high school' scripts I was reading. It captured the disaffected, restless spirit of youth, while tackling some very mature themes that, if I'm honest, were somewhat over my head at the time.

To me, *Deadgirl* felt like a modern western. Not through its physical landscape, but through its internal moral one; a tale of two friends at a crossroads, headed toward an old-fashioned showdown. Rickie and JT's battle between morality and impulse, loyalty and betrayal, mirrored the traditional western's clash between civilization and the wild frontier. It offered what, I believe, all great films should: a surface-level thrill that harbors an undercurrent of profound meaning…for those brave enough to dive beneath the chilled waters.

After I was cast, I made a strange request to my agent: "Can I meet the writer?" Typically, my first instinct is to talk to the director so I can better understand their vision and how they plan to craft the film's world. With *Deadgirl*, however, the essence of Trent's script felt like the core of the project. I needed to connect with the mind behind those words, to try and understand the nuances, and perhaps the madness, that went into crafting such a complex narrative. It was clear to me that while the brilliant directors, Gadi Harel and Marcel Sarmiento, would shape the visual storytelling, the heart and soul of this film resided in Trent's script. (Trent was also the assistant director, and his wife, Lynh, was the costume designer. Angels, both of them).

Casting JT, my best friend turned rival, was pivotal, and Noah Segan was the perfect man for the job. I lived in Venice Beach, and he lived just north of me, so we were close enough to spend a lot of time together. (Los Angeles is a sprawling city, and it takes at least an hour to get anywhere).

Noah is one of a kind. He's a wordsmith. He's tough. He's hilarious, and he's fearless. I loved his work in *Brick* and was captivated by his unique spirit. We talked about our characters, and he filled me in on the allegories the film represented. I learned and grew as an actor. Watching Noah perform as JT was enlightening. He understands film acting and brought subtleties to JT that were understated on set, yet monumental on screen. His is one of the best performances I've had the pleasure of witnessing, and his Fright Meter Award for Best Actor was well deserved (though I believe he should have won an Oscar, as well).

The stark transformation of *Deadgirl's* tone from set to screen was astounding. The locations were grim and the makeup haunting. But it was the film's dark, horror-infused aesthetic that was a revelation. The cinematography, editing, and sound design all worked together to create an oppressive, chilling environment that seeped into my bones.

The exploration into the depths of human morality and depravity was far more visceral and disturbing than I had imagined while shooting. My surprise wasn't just about the genre; it was about understanding how much a film can evolve through collaborative efforts in post-production. It taught me that a film is not just made on set; it's reborn through the visionary work of all those who touch it long after the cameras stop rolling. The experience underscored the magic and mystery of filmmaking…where the final product can be a beautiful, haunting surprise, even to those who lived through its creation.

Which brings me to this book. Bridgett Nelson's novelization delves deeper into the world Trent created, and I am thrilled that she took on this project. Her transformation of the film is an exciting new chapter for our *Deadgirl*. Her writing fills out the world we all dared to build those years ago—the provocative, unflinching themes, conflicts, and haunting questions that lingered long after the original story ended. She has masterfully expanded the narrative, revealing aspects of the story that are only hinted at in the movie. Her adaptation delves into the psychological and moral complexities that the film could only touch upon, offering a richer, more nuanced exploration of the characters and their world. I believe this novel will resonate more powerfully today as society grapples with increasingly polarized debates about ethics, consent, and the essence of human nature.

I'm immensely grateful for *Deadgirl*. It wasn't just another acting gig; it was a formative chapter in my life, teaching me the immense power of storytelling. It not only gave me lifelong friends, but experiences that fundamentally shaped my career.

Deadgirl is raw, real, and unapologetically bold—a story that dared to be different. That it still resonates with people feels like validation for our brave little crew.

To those who've watched the film and can't wait to read the novelization…thank you for being part of our adventure. I hope you feel the same connection to this story that I've felt since that long-ago day on Wilshire Boulevard. The narrative, now reborn in the pages of this book, invites us all into a continuous conversation about what it means to be human…one I'm honored to share with you.

While MapQuest has faded into history, the journey with *Deadgirl* continues.

Shiloh Fernandez, "Rickie"
Los Angeles, California
December 2024

FOREWORD

"JT"

NOAH SEGAN

Deadgirl is a comedy. It's hilarious. A chuckle a minute. So many laughs, I dare you to catch a breath.

That's what I told myself while preparing to film it. Trent Haaga's brilliant script had its share of wit, cynicism, and satire. But like the greats—Voltaire, Terry Southern, Elaine May—there was a biting truth, pun intended, that scared me.

I play a lot of bad guys. Often, guys who are bad at being bad. As an actor, that's my revenge—to show that villains are bullies. That if we can laugh at them, we take away their power. If we can put a spotlight on a villain's vulnerabilities, they *might* become more dangerous, but they might also become more manageable…understandable. It's the flashlight under the bed. It's coping through comedy.

Much of that justification wasn't available for me with JT— no matter how pitiful or cringey I made him, I couldn't make up for what he does. If you relate to him, you're fucked. Into the trashcan you go. My coping mechanism was limited, so I tried to take solace that the film would do the work. That my colleagues' humanity would speak to the point of the story, the moral. Luckily, we had Shiloh, so soulful and tender and tight. And Jenny, who maintained fierceness and used every one of her character's limitations as an expressive tool.

Shooting was a whirlwind. I'd been living in a rented room but had recently found my own place. I used the production as an excuse to live in an empty apartment I didn't know, with few comforts, in a neighborhood across town. Thoroughly untrained, this wasn't some kind of method acting self-flagellation, but a way of shutting off my brain after long days of being the worst dude ever. I'd like to think that leaning into the sarcastic, punchline-y tone of Trent's dialogue was another way to protect my own momma's boy mentality.

Super low budget, we didn't have the trappings of trailers or time between set-ups and scenes. We just shot and shot for three straight weeks. There wasn't time to consider the reality of what I was doing, and that was a good thing. What was on the page went on the stage, as they say. I didn't question it, because I knew the scumbag I was playing wasn't thinking two steps ahead either. In a way, life was imitating art.

Deadgirl is, thankfully, an artifact. With the novelization, it shows even further how far we've come in the way we treat each other, especially women—the risks we take in traumatizing them through our ignorance and misogyny. The macho lust for power corrupts absolutely.

Like the film, Bridgett's work tracks a slippery slope from disenfranchised, vulnerable people to the unimaginable horrors they're put through. What Bridgett has done, through Ivy's story, is humanize a character whose humanity was stolen. In doing so, she added a new layer of horror, but also one of sympathy. This novelization, and its backstory, are studies in the cycles of trauma. We've come far in terms of what we expect from our boys, and how we teach our children to treat one another. Not far enough, obviously, but as we evolve, this film and novelization will hopefully serve more as a fable than a cautionary tale.

Noah Segan, "JT"
Los Angeles, California
January 2025

To Shiloh, Noah, Jenny, and Trent. Getting to know each of you has been the highlight of this project. Thanks for being awesome!

DEADGIRL

1

NOW

The door might as well have been a wall.

It stood, impenetrable, the uneven metal surface gleaming softly in the dim basement lighting. Flaky, brick-red rust like ancient, dried blood. The tarnished knob hung loosely in the door's bore hole, completely useless, yet somehow mocking.

"Door's not locked, just rusted shut. Push!" JT said, hands flat against the cold steel, as Rickie joined him. "Push, boy!"

Nothing happened.

"Fuck!" Moving some antiquated medical equipment aside, JT sifted impatiently through the debris on the floor.

"Maybe we should just go, JT. How're we gonna get in?" Rickie asked, searching with his fingers along the swollen wooden door frame.

This was not at all how he'd expected to spend the afternoon after ditching school. Having a few beers? Sure. Exploring the sub-basement of the local, condemned nuthouse? Not so much.

"With this," JT answered with a grin, lifting a length of rusted pipe. "The end is flattened like a damn pancake. I think it'll work." He wedged it into the doorjamb and pushed, grunting with exertion. "Help me out here, man!"

Four hands gripped the rough, corroded pipe as frustrated

growls echoed throughout the subterranean corridor. Putting their full weight behind the makeshift crowbar, the door gave slightly but didn't open.

"Push, fer Chrissake! Put your back into it. We've almost got it!" JT yelled.

Rickie's muscles strained with the effort. This was a job for the jocks, and he and JT were most assuredly *not* jocks. They were both thin and lanky, the guys from the wrong side of the tracks, who'd been bullied and picked on since elementary school.

Rickie had olive skin and shaggy brown hair that flopped casually to the side. His eyes were dark brown and piercing, but not in a way that attracted girls. He lived in t-shirts and a faded army jacket and was far more interested in comic books and art than football.

JT wore whatever he could find at the local Goodwill—usually jeans and tank tops, with black combat boots and a thin, well-loved hoodie. His light brown hair was styled in a greased-back pompadour/mullet hybrid that emphasized his pale, blue-eyed features.

With a loud metallic clang and a showering of dust, the door creaked open. To Rickie, it sounded creepy…like a warning. JT haughtily threw the pipe to the ground, staring intently at him —an obvious dare—before crossing the threshold. "C'mon, Rickie," he said, pushing stained and shredded plastic sheeting aside.

Rickie scanned the area behind him, fingers clutching the door frame, then hesitantly entered the room. JT strode confidently into the darkness, disappearing around a corner.

"JT, what the fuck you doing, man?" He eased his way deeper into the space, eyes adjusting to the thick shadows, gripping various dripping pipes along the way to prevent himself from falling. The pipework extended to the ceiling, zigzagging above his head. "Is this like some kind of boiler room?"

"Dunno." JT's voice was muffled.

"Hey…" Rickie started.

JT cut him off with a startled yelp. "Holy shit!"

"JT, what the hell?" Rickie asked. "What's going on? You okay?"

"Holy shit," JT responded again, dumbfounded.

"What? Dammit, talk to me, man!" Rickie said, slowly making his way onward.

"You're never going to believe this." An undercurrent of excitement tinged the words.

He wasn't wrong.

As Rickie turned the corner and the image before him became clear, all he could do was stare incredulously. "*Holy shit*, man," he whispered, unable to look away.

"Yeah, I told you," JT said, a satisfied grin stretching across his narrow face.

Rickie took a deep breath, gaping at the plastic-shrouded, naked girl chained to an old hospital gurney, and asked the obvious question.

"What the *fuck* is she doing down here?"

THEN

"I like girls," I blurted, mouth dry, hands shaking.

The darkness was heavy in the bedroom I shared with my twin sister. I couldn't see Lily's face, but I knew exactly how it looked at that moment—because it was also mine—the same shoulder-length medium-brown hair, uptilted nose, espresso-colored eyes, wide smile, and pointy chin. Our annoying little brother once told us we looked like praying mantises. *Asshole*.

Right now, Lily's eyes would be closed, her cheeks flushed with the pressure of the situation, and she'd be gently chewing on her lip as she considered her response. She was not an impulsive person. Quiet, thoughtful, easy-going…that was Lily. I, on the other hand, was a little…louder.

Chilled, despite the warm, early-summer air seeping through our open window, I pulled the lavender and yellow quilt that graced our shared full-sized bed to my chin. I'd wanted a red and black one, but Mom refused to make it.

"Those are Jezebel colors, Ivy Elizabeth!" she'd said with a chuckle.

Bed springs creaked as Lily rolled to her side, exhaling a pent-up breath. "I know, Ivy. I know you do. I figured it out a long time ago. Back when you and Eva used to sneak off by yourselves all the time. I saw you kissing her behind the winery once. I guess I just hoped it was a stage you'd grow out of." The worry in her voice was evident. "You can't let Daddy find out."

I sighed, knowing she was right. Our father, Edgar Reyes, Napa Valley vineyard owner and deacon of the local church, was overbearing and strict. He kept all of us, including my mom and three siblings, on a very short leash. Not that having evangelical Christian parents ever stopped me. "Daddy is a tyrant, and I can't imagine anything good happening if he finds out, but right now, I'm more worried about how you feel. *You're* my person."

Lily's hand found mine beneath the blankets. Its soft warmth was comforting. "You know I only want you to be happy, Poison." Lily had called me 'Poison Ivy' since our grade school days. "I just worry you'll be found out. Daddy would disown you, and Mama would cry for days. If suicide wasn't such a deadly sin, that's probably what she'd do. You'll break their hearts."

"But what about my heart, Tiger Lily? I can't live my life for them." I shifted, unable to get comfortable, then gave my down pillow a few frustrated punches for good measure. "Am I supposed to marry a man just to make them happy?"

"No, of course not. But you know they're going to expect grandchildren. We're women." She deepened her voice to sound like our dad. "It's all we're good for." Lily shifted onto her back, staring at the ceiling. When she finally spoke, her voice quivered. "This is not going to be an easy path. I'm scared for you."

"Don't be scared. You know I'll be fine no matter what." I said it with more bravado than I felt.

Lily chuckled. "Ivy Elizabeth Reyes…the wild, crazy, outgoing, over-the-top twin who always comes out on top."

"You're fucking right," I said, wrapping my arm around Lily's waist and resting my head on her shoulder.

"Oh my gosh, that's horrible! Don't say that word, Poison! It's so raunchy."

"Fuckity fuck, fuckfuckfuck!"

Lily good-naturedly pushed me away as she giggled. "You're so bad!"

Smiling and relieved by the way our discussion had gone, I rolled over, plumping my pillow and snuggling the blanket. Before I drifted off to sleep, I whispered, "Love you, Tiger."

"Love you too, Poison."

3

NOW

Rickie couldn't take his eyes off the girl. "Is she…you think she's fuckin'…?" He couldn't finish the thought.

JT stepped forward. "Only one way to find out." He reached toward her unmoving body.

Rickie fidgeted, holding his breath, watching JT's fingers move closer and closer to what he could only assume was a fresh corpse.

The girl took a single breath, causing the plastic to suck back into her mouth. JT jumped backward in surprise, shouting a high-pitched, "Holy shit! Ho-ly shiiit!"

Rickie ran his hands through his hair in disbelief. "What the fuck is she doing down here? Oh my God!"

"She didn't just tie herself to that fucking bed, man, that's for sure."

Rickie edged toward the door, wary of some hidden kidnapper. "Well, we better get outta here, man. Go to the cops. What if whoever did this decides to come back? We gotta get the fuck outta here *now*."

"Sh-sh-sh-sh-sh-sh-sh!" JT waved for him to be quiet with one hand, while looking intently around the room. "Just hold on a sec, Rick."

Throwing out his arms in frustration, Rickie replied, "Are you fucking out of your mind? There's a fucking naked woman down here, bro! Let's just go."

As if suddenly realizing the significance of their find, JT barked out a laugh, "Hot damn."

"This isn't funny, dude. We gotta get out of here!" Rickie said, nervously pacing.

JT leaned forward, studying the girl. "Will you take it easy, man? Just hold on a second. I need to think."

"Take it easy? We're in the basement of a fucking nuthouse with a naked, kidnapped woman! What the fuck, man? Take it easy?"

"Fucking chill out for a second, will ya?" He didn't take his eyes off the girl. Seconds passed before he spoke again. "We had to pry that door open. You saw it yourself. It was rusted shut, right?"

"Yeah, but maybe there's another way in."

"And not just a little rusted shut...that thing probably hadn't been opened for years. There's nobody down here, man. We've been raising hell here all day. We're alone. There's nobody here but us."

Rickie thought about their activities that afternoon...the fire alarm at school that caused them to ditch the rest of their classes; the way his unrequited crush, JoAnn, smiled at him when she retrieved the inhaler her asshole boyfriend had thrown over her head; riding their bikes to the nuthouse...followed by endless beer, destruction, graffiti, and laughter. They'd been there for hours before finding the door in the sub-basement, and not once had they come across anyone else. The place felt long abandoned. And if there was another way into the room, Rickie had yet to find it.

"All right. We're alone. Good, man, good. Now let's free the fucking girl and get the fuck out of here, please." The words rushed from his mouth in a panicked barrage.

In response, JT grasped the filthy plastic and slowly pulled it down the girl's bare body, uncovering her breasts and whiskey-colored nipples. Her skin was covered in dirt and grime.

"Dude, don't," Rickie pleaded. "Cut it out." He grabbed JT's arm when he refused to stop. *"Cut it the fuck out!"*

"Hey!" Irritated, JT yanked away from Rickie's grip. The look he gave him was anything but friendly. "Will you just shut up for half a goddamn second? Jesus!"

Rickie tried another angle. "JT, man, maybe some girl has been missing, right? I mean, there could be some kind of reward or something, you know?"

"We could keep her," JT said quietly, his voice intense.

Appalled, Rickie said, *"What?* JT, man. Keep her?"

"Just for tonight. Or tomorrow." He leered over her body.

"JT...*keep* her?

"Look at her, man. She's like a model in a magazine."

"What are you talking about, man? Are you fucking kidding? Let's go!"

"I could spend all day looking at that body," JT responded, a small smile playing on his lips.

"Jesus fucking Christ!"

JT was too busy ogling the girl to react to his disgust. "She is *beautiful.*"

"I mean, Jesus, JT...this is stupid, man." Rickie's voice crackled with emotion. "We gotta free the girl and get the fuck out of here. *Please*, man. I'm begging you."

JT poked his finger into the side of her breast.

"What are you doing, man?" Rickie said, grimacing. "Come on, knock it off."

"Oh, that's *nice*," JT said. "You gotta come feel that." Rickie had never seen him look happier. "Come here and feel this titty, man."

The girl's long-lashed, red-rimmed eyes fluttered as JT caressed her breast. Her mouth opened, exposing teeth blackened at the gumline.

Rickie shook his head, exhaling. "There's no way I'm gonna fucking…"

"Your loss," JT cut him off, greedily eyeing the girl.

Rickie grasped his shoulder as he reached again for her breast. "JT, cut it out. Seriously. That's not cool, bro."

"Get the fuck off me," JT said, twisting away from his hand. His stare was cold, hard.

"No. You're better than this, JT," Rickie said, pulling him from the girl.

JT turned toward him, fists raised.

"What the fuck are you doing?" he asked, stunned.

By way of answer, JT reared back and punched him in the mouth.

Stumbling backward and cradling his face, Rickie yelled, "What the fuck, JT? What the fuck has gotten into you, man?"

JT shrugged, unapologetic. "What the fuck's gotten into *you*? Why you suddenly acting like some faggot?" He sneered at the blood dripping from Rickie's lip. "Look at her, man. Just look at that chick."

"You're fucking sick, man. I'm getting the fuck out of here, and you're coming with me."

JT pointed a warning finger at him. "Get the fuck back, man. You can sit around lusting over JoAnn Skinner all you want, but I'm fucking sick and tired of settling for drunken cows at keggers. This chick…is fucking *hot!* We'd be idiots to pass this up! She's like a fucking Christmas present all wrapped up and waiting for us. Or should I say…*unwrapped?*" He chuckled. "But seriously, fucking *look* at her, Rickie! We hit the lottery!"

Rickie glanced at the helpless, vulnerable woman, then back at JT. "I can't fucking believe you, man. I thought you were better than this."

"You were wrong," JT said. "You don't want her? Fine. Just go. Get the hell outta here." He motioned to the door. "You were never here as far as I'm concerned."

"You can't do this. I won't let you."

JT whipped around and flung another punch at Rickie's face, knocking him to the ground. "Go on," he growled. "Go on. Just get! Get outta here."

Rickie pulled himself up and walked away.

4

THEN

"Violet, Lily, Ivy, Robert! Time for dinner!"

I heard my siblings eagerly plow down the stairs. Momma had made navy bean soup with cornbread, a family favorite. It had been simmering all day, whetting our appetites. For dessert, grape pie. Living on a vineyard, you'd think we'd be sick of grapes, but none of us ever were. Maybe it was because Momma knew which type of grape was best suited to which dessert, based on their texture and flavor. She was a culinary magician.

I sighed contentedly as I listened to the comforting sounds emanating from the dining room…the clanging of pots and pans, the gurgle of milk being poured into six glasses, the light 'ting' of spoons hitting bowls. My belly grumbled. But instead of running downstairs, I nestled into the rocking chair in our bedroom and continued my diary entry, wanting to get these feelings that were bursting from inside of me onto paper.

Carrie and I spent the evening on the hill overlooking the vineyard. It was far enough away that I didn't worry about anyone seeing us, but close enough that I could keep an eye on things. She's smart and funny and beautiful and wants to go to New York City to be an actress after we graduate. I have no idea what I want to do yet, but NYC sounds fun. We laughed so hard together, and every time I heard her giggle, I wanted nothing more than to kiss those sweet, pouty lips of hers.

When I finally did, she kissed me back! I'm so happy, diary. I've never felt like this before. I think she may be the one…

"Where the hell is Ivy?" I heard Daddy bellow. He may have been a religious man, but it didn't stop him from cursing like a sailor. "Tell her to get her ass down here before I get the switch."

"I'll get her," Lily said, trying to appease him. Seconds later, her light, brisk steps rushed up the stairs.

"No child of mine will be so damned disrespectful of her momma's hard work," I heard Daddy grumble.

Hiding my diary beneath the loose floorboard behind the rocking chair, I met Lily at the door.

"You'd better come. Daddy is in a *mood*. I have half a notion to ask if it's his time of the month." Lily rolled her eyes.

That was one of the many things I loved about my twin. She was a rule-follower to the core, but she had a healthy dose of sarcasm and used it liberally when the moment was right. Though not toward our father. *Never* toward our father.

"I was on my way down. Just woke up from a little nap."

She glanced at my hiding spot in the corner, then looked at me with knowing eyes.

"Bet it was a lovely nap."

"The very best." We giggled as we ran down the stairs and settled ourselves into our seats at the dinner table.

"Well, well, well. Look who finally decided to grace us with her presence." Daddy had a piece of cornbread stuck in his beard. I didn't tell him. He was a large man—not fat, but not muscular either. Just sort of…mushy. His dark, slicked-back hair accented beady eyes, a wide nose, and thin lips.

"Yes, so sorry about that, Daddy." I clutched my lower abdomen. "I started my monthly curse, and I was getting cleaned up in the bathroom. It's just so messy, you know? And I feel so swollen and uncomfortable, especially my breasts. Plus, it usually makes my bowels act up and…"

"Er, okay, okay. That's enough, Ivy." Daddy looked a little green. "Just apologize to your momma for being late."

"Sorry for my angry uterus, Momma!" I gave her my biggest, brightest grin as Lily stifled her laughter.

"It's fine, it's fine." I saw mirth in her eyes. I suspected my momma, Rosemary, who looked like a slightly older version of Lily and me, had behaved very much like me when she was younger—outspoken and butting heads with far less intelligent males. How she ended up tied to a buffoon like my father, I'll never know. "Just give me your bowl so I can fill it for you."

As we ate, Daddy held court, as always. "Despite this cursed war, people are desperate to spend their hard-earned money indulging in libations to ease their pains." He took a big bite of beans and continued talking with his mouth full. "It's 1945, after all, and time for things to change. So a group of us have started the Napa Valley Vintners Association. Soon, Reyes' wines will be on shelves all across the country."

"That's wonderful, Dad," Violet said. "Good for you!"

Violet, the oldest, was a shameless ass-kisser, and, according to anyone with eyes, far less pretty than my twin and me. She and Robert were mini replicas of our father.

"Thank you, darlin'. It was all my idea."

I doubted that. As far as I could tell, the only two things Daddy was good at were growing grapes and controlling his family with an iron fist. He didn't have a mind for business, though Momma did. I suspected this venture was her idea.

"You're so smart!" Violet was destined to be a spinster. Nobody would ever live up to Daddy in her eyes.

"Indeed, he is. Proud of you, honey," Momma said, giving his forearm a brisk rub. But not before offering me a brief wink. I turned to hide my smile.

"Can I have more beans?" Robert, the baby of the family, ate more than all three of us girls combined. "Another piece of cornbread, too!"

"I'll join you, son," Dad said, passing his bowl to Momma. God forbid he got off his ass and served himself.

"Don't you think you both should say 'please?'" I glared at my father and brother, sick of their disgusting manners.

Daddy returned my glare, not moving a muscle, but Robert didn't hold back. "It's what women are good for. Right, Dad?"

He sounded just like Daddy. I felt a twinge of sadness for some nice girl, who right now was enjoying a lovely dinner with her own family, not knowing she was destined to marry my shithead little brother.

Daddy clenched his fists at my insolence, and Momma, sensing the brewing battle, hopped up with a smile and served their second portions. "There we go. All good. Would anyone else like anything?" We declined, but the rest of the meal was quiet and awkward.

Over dessert, Daddy asked, "What's everyone's plans for the rest of this fine summer evening?"

"I'd love to play a game of chess with you, Daddy," Violet chimed in.

"Of course, dear. Perhaps I'll try out our new Pinot Noir while we play. Just be sure to take it easy on your old man." His laughter boomed across the room, as if the idea of a girl—his daughter, no less—beating him was absurd. "Robert, how about you?"

"I'm gonna ride my bike to Theo's house and play baseball."

"Sounds like a fine idea. Lily?"

Lily hated being the center of attention. She looked down at her plate. "I have a new book I'd like to read. It's supposed to be really good."

"Hm. I guess that's okay for today..." Daddy stroked his bearded chin. "...but you really need to get outside more."

"I was planning to have a picnic lunch with her tomorrow, Daddy. She'll get some sun," I said, jumping to Lily's defense.

"Excellent." Daddy shifted in his seat and glowered at me. "And what are *you* doing tonight, Ivy?"

"Oh, I was planning to take a walk, you know? Do some exploring now that it's cooled down a bit."

I had plans with Carrie.

"While that sounds like a fine idea, the horses need a good rub-down. Take care of it, please."

And there it was. My punishment for being late to dinner and embarrassing him in front of the family by challenging his manners.

"Yes, Daddy," I choked out.

He nodded and smiled smugly, then turned to Momma.

Without waiting for him to ask, she said, "The kids need some warmer clothes for the winter, so I'll be on the back porch knitting."

"I request you avoid that hideous, drab gray color you used last year. It made us all look like prisoners."

"I use what I can get, Edgar."

"Then get better."

"Yes, dear."

Daddy clapped his hands in rapid succession. "You're all dismissed."

I knew it was a sin in God's eyes—like most of the things I did in my life—but hopefully God understood why I absolutely loathed the man who fathered me.

5

NOW

Rickie rode his bike home under ominous skies...skies that matched his mood. *Fucking JT.* He passed the 'Welcome to Evansburgh, California – A Nice Slice of Paradise' sign without acknowledging it and sped past sleazy strip malls, broken down cars, greasy fast-food joints, and neglected houses, before parking in front of yet another run-down home.

Inside, he headed straight for the black, wall-mounted phone in their lived-in kitchen. His mom worked hard, but never could save enough to buy him a cell phone. "Ma, you home?" he called out. There was only silence. Rickie picked up the phone, dialed, and listened to it ring twice before he heard a female voice say, "911. What's your emergency?"

"*Damn*, boy, what happened to your face?"

Startled, Rickie jumped and slammed the receiver down into the cradle. A large man, wearing a dirty white t-shirt and an even dirtier chambray button-down over his paunchy beer gut, loomed over him. What little hair he had was styled in a comb-over.

"Where's my mom?"

"She picked up an extra shift. Said she'd be home around

midnight," he said, taking a long draw of the Tall Boy Bud in his hand.

"Yeah, well, what are you doing here…*Clint?*"

Rickie hated the guy. Everyone in town knew Clint was a piece of shit. He'd abandoned his own kids, leaving them with their mother, forgetting they existed, and offering no financial support. Not surprising behavior from a guy who clearly didn't understand the purpose of the washing machine. Or deodorant.

Swallowing the brew with a loud gulp, Clint replied, "Your mom said it would be all right if I, uh…" he bobbed his head drunkenly, "…stuck around for a few weeks."

Annoyed by his mother's persistent need to have a man around, especially a half-wit, hick like this one, Rickie couldn't help but roll his eyes.

Clint, ignoring Rickie's obvious displeasure, studied his black eye and split lip, grinned, and said, "Man, I hope you gave as good as you got."

Here we go, Rickie thought, bracing for Clint's inevitable bullshit speech. He liked to pretend he was Rickie's father, often doling out his brand of 'fatherly' advice.

"You gotta stand up to these bastards and give it to them worse than they gave it to you, ya know? In this world, you can't let other people fight your battles for ya. It's called T-C-B, Rickie. Yeah? *Takin' care of business.*"

Rickie mouthed the last few words along with Clint, his face red with anger and humiliation. "That's great fucking advice, Clint," he said with a smirk. "I mean, thank you. Especially coming from a fucking alcoholic who can't even pay his fucking rent. Hey! Why don't you drink some more of my mom's beers and then tell me about being a *real* man, huh?"

"Come on, Rickie," Clint slurred, waving his beer around. "Why the attitude? I'm just trying to help you."

"Yeah, well, gee whiz, Clint…thank you." Rickie stomped toward his bedroom.

"You know what?" Clint yelled after him. "It was your

goddamned mom's idea for me to talk to you in the first place! But I know all the talking in the world ain't gonna make *you* a man." Rickie's door slammed shut, but he kept yelling. "You gotta do it yourself! Fuckin' kids." He belched, then took another long swig of the beer.

6

THEN

I stumbled down the gravel road, determined not to fall. When a shape jumped in front of me, I screamed like a banshee, then couldn't stop giggling when I realized it was a little, fluffy bunny and not a bobcat, or some other dangerous predator.

"Aren't you a cutie! I just wanna snuggle you and eat you right up!" I declared.

The bunny stared at me, frozen in fear. I bent to pick it up, then watched it hop frantically into the woods as I fell face-first onto the soft grass lining the lane.

"Oopsie daisy!" I said, laughing as blood trickled from my nose.

I wasn't feeling any pain. My body was numbed by the liberal amounts of alcohol I'd had during the party...the party Daddy had specifically forbidden us to attend.

Staggering to my feet, I walked on, feeling the warm blood drip down my face, and taking deep, cleansing breaths to try and sober up. When our house appeared in the distance, I clumsily hurried toward it, wanting nothing more than to crawl into the bed I shared with Lily, and slip into oblivion, thinking about the way Carrie had touched my body earlier.

Reaching the edge of our yard, I paused, and did my best to

fight the effects of the alcohol in my system. I needed to *quietly* sneak into our bedroom. Lily, who'd opted not to go to the party, had promised to leave the window unlocked. I crept across the lawn, feeling steadier. When I reached the tree, I looked up, studying the branches and the path I'd take that would bring me right to the window. Under normal circumstances, I could do it with my eyes closed, but this wasn't normal circumstances. I was kinda trashed.

Or, you know…*a lot* trashed.

Bracing my foot against the first limb, I pulled myself up. Then again. And again. *This is going great! What was I so worried about? I am a lioness! Stealthy, agile, strong, Hear me roar!*

I climbed onto the final branch, just outside our bedroom window. Clambering through it, I fell headfirst over the sill…straight into Daddy's arms.

He dropped me unceremoniously onto the floor. In a quiet, menacing voice, he ordered, "Lily, go get your sister a glass of water. Ivy, get your ass into the rocking chair."

Lily gave me a look I couldn't quite interpret and raced from the room.

"Edgar, why don't you let me take care of this?" Momma had appeared in the doorway, glancing at my bloody face with concern.

"Go back to bed, Rosie. I've got it. I'll be along shortly." Daddy never took his eyes off me.

"What's going on?" Robert said, coming out of his room and rubbing his sleep-crusted eyes.

Momma gently pushed him back. "Nothing, honey. Come on. I'll get you tucked back in."

Violet smirked at me from the shadows of the hallway. She loved when her siblings got into trouble. It made her look better, like the 'good' kid…our parents' favorite.

She wished.

"Here, Daddy," Lily said, handing him a large cup of water.

"Get back into bed, Lily." He gave me the cool glass. "Drink. All of it. Now."

The tone of his voice left no room for argument, so I chugged it all, not realizing until that moment how thirsty I was.

"How much alcohol did you drink tonight, Ivy?"

I held my head defiantly, looking him in the eye. "Lots."

"Not surprising." He scoffed. "We heard you jabbering to yourself as you climbed the tree. Incoherent rambling—and something about a lioness—followed by loud giggles."

Huh. I thought I'd been super sneaky.

"Did you even notice you have sticks and leaves in your hair?"

I touched my scalp, felt the offending items, and snort-laughed. Guess I wasn't as stealthy as I thought.

"Get ready for bed, Ivy." His voice was tight. I could tell he was fighting for control of his anger. "We'll talk more about this in the morning when you've sobered up. But just know that you're grounded for the next six months, and if I ever discover you've been drinking again, there will be far more severe consequences. Do you understand?"

Ready to make a snide remark, I saw Lily's pale face in the lamplight. She mouthed, "No," and wildly shook her head.

"I unther…" I blinked, trying to focus. My lips and tongue didn't seem to be working. "I understand." I stood, tottering, and started toward the bathroom. As I walked past Daddy, he gave me a hard shove, knocking me forcefully to the floor.

Kneeling beside me, he said, "I'm sick of your bullshit, Ivy." His breath was sour…hot and fetid on my face. It made me queasy. "Be more like your sisters and straighten the fuck up."

Feeling suddenly sober and pissed beyond belief, I was unable to help myself as I blurted. "If you think I'll ever be an ass-kissing sycophant like Violet, you don't know me at all."

"Ivy, no!" Lily yelled, distraught.

I watched as Daddy's face suffused with blood, the veins in

his forehead throbbing. He slapped my cheek so hard, my head snapped violently to the right, and my skull thudded against the hardwood floor.

"Watch your mouth, girl. Just watch your damn mouth." He stood, eyeing me as he did. "There is something wrong with you, Ivy. Something very wrong. And we're gonna fix it."

The door slammed shut behind him. I grasped my throbbing face and cried. Lily wrapped her arms around my chest and rocked me until I fell asleep.

7

NOW

At dusk, Rickie stole an old .22 pistol from Clint's glove compartment, and walked to a nearby freeway underpass, filled with discarded mattresses, old, rusted appliances, and a giant dumpster that reeked of rotten eggs, cabbage, and stale piss.

Aiming at an ancient washing machine lying on its side, he fired five shots. The slight recoil caused the throbbing in his bloodied and bruised face to worsen.

Footsteps echoed across the blacktop. "Hope you're not seeing my face when you pull that trigger," JT joked.

Rickie, still in the shooter's stance, glanced briefly at him but didn't respond.

"Rickie! C'mon, man! We've been friends for too long. Don't shut me out now."

Lowering his arms, Rickie looked at JT. "Yeah, I thought we were friends, too. Right up until the moment you fuckin' punched me."

JT had the decency to look ashamed. "I'm sorry about that, all right?"

"And what about her? You sorry about that too?"

"That's why I came down here," JT answered. "I need you to go back there with me, man."

"Are you fucking serious? She's still down there?"

JT said nothing.

"Right now?"

JT nodded.

Rickie shook his head. "No way, man. Fucking forget it."

"Rickie, please, man. *Please.* There's something you gotta see. It's important. Nah, it's *really* important."

"If it's so important, why don't you just tell me right here?"

"Cuz you gotta see it! Man, you wouldn't believe me if I just told you."

"No." Rickie shook his head again. "No, man. I don't wanna be an accessory to whatever sick shit you're doing."

"I wouldn't ask if it wasn't a big deal. You *have* to see this."

Torn, Rickie's gaze shifted from JT to the washing machine and back to JT again.

"Rickie, *please.*"

"You're an asshole." Sighing, Rickie aimed and fired another round into the abandoned washing machine before tucking the gun into his pocket.

* * *

He walked back to the house, JT following. As they got near, they saw a cop car pulling into the driveway.

"What are the fucking cops doing here, Rickie?" JT hissed as an officer ambled to the front door and knocked. "Did you call the fucking cops?"

Rickie said nothing, just watched as a drunk, belligerent Clint answered the door. They couldn't hear what was being said, but the conversation quickly turned heated. Clint took a swing at the cop, who easily dodged it, and had Clint on the ground and in handcuffs in mere seconds.

"Your mom's boyfriend is a real class act," JT said as Clint yelled drunken slurs at the officer. "Just think, someday, he could be your daddy."

"Are we going, or not?" Rickie asked.

"Changed your mind?"

"Let's just get on our bikes and go, okay?"

* * *

Rickie berated himself as he pedaled toward the nuthouse. If he were smart, he'd turn around and head straight home, but…he was curious. And also oddly determined to see this through. The girl had only him in her corner.

JT used a flashlight to illuminate the mold-stained, peeling walls as they walked through the dark, shadowy hallways of the old hospital. When the sub-basement door finally came into view, Rickie, who had been silent throughout the entirety of the trip, said, "We're letting her go, JT. Okay? That's all there is to it, man. And hopefully she doesn't send your ass to jail."

JT pushed the creaking barrier open. "She's not going to send me to jail." His voice was confident.

"Why not? I mean, what did you do to her?" Rickie's voice grew louder. "What the *fuck* did you do to her, man?" Frustrated, he looked away, whispering under his breath. "You're fucking killing me…"

JT motioned for Rickie to enter the room.

"No fuckin' way."

JT leaned against the doorframe, shoulders sagging, hands hanging uselessly by his sides. He looked guilty as hell.

"Just tell me what you did to her, man," Rickie's voice cracked with emotion.

When JT spoke, his voice was soft. "She woke up as I was fucking her." His jaw clenched. "She started to struggle, of course, but she didn't scream. No. She just sort of…growled. And she tried to bite like a wild fucking dog, ya know? So, I, uh…I hit her."

Rickie's breathing became ragged.

"Just enough to make her stop, you know?" JT continued.

"Oh, man." Rickie couldn't look at him. How the hell could he talk so matter-of-factly about physically abusing a helpless young woman?

"But she didn't. She surely did *not* stop, Rickie. She just kept gnashing at me with those teeth." He paused, then quietly went on. "So I hit her again…and it felt *good*. Really good. I kept punching her and punching her, and it just made me harder. I don't know what came over me, man. I've never felt anything like it. And my punches didn't have any effect on her. She just kept snapping at me and growling like a fucking dog. I loved it." JT had the decency to act ashamed. "But you wouldn't know about that."

"You're damn right I wouldn't." Rickie's fists curled. "Jesus Christ."

"Then I hit her harder…"

"Who the fuck *are* you? Because you're sure as hell not the JT I know. And what the fuck did you do, man?"

"…and harder and harder."

"Jesus, JT." Rickie knew he sounded like a disapproving parent but didn't care.

"I was so turned on, I wrapped my hands around her neck and just…did it, you know? After a while, she stopped moving."

"For Christ's sake, man, you fucking *killed* her? You sick fuck! What the fuck were you thinking, JT? You fucking kill this poor girl, and you bring me down here to show me a fucking corpse?"

"I thought I broke her."

"Broke her? *Broke* her? She's not a fucking toy, fer Chrissake! Lemme in!"

"Rickie!" JT tried to stop him, but Rickie pushed his way past.

"You're a sick fuck! I've had enough of your psycho shit." He strode to the gurney. "We're taking her out of here now, man."

"Hold on a sec," JT said, following Rickie.

"No, this has gone far enough!" He reached for the shackles, staring at the girl's limp, bruised body.

"You still have to see what I brought you here for."

Noticing the dark, purple bruises surrounding her neck, he said, "I've seen *more* than enough, JT. Fuck, man."

Without warning, JT pulled the .22 from the pocket of Rickie's faded green army jacket. "No, you haven't, Rickie." He pointed the gun at him. "Not yet."

"What the fuck are you doing?" Rickie placed a hand over his abdomen, as if it would protect him from a bullet. "Put the gun down, man!"

The girl turned her head, opened dull, bloodshot eyes, and looked at them. There was a smudge of dirt on the tip of her pert nose.

"You ain't seen nothing yet!" JT turned the gun toward her.

"No, man, no!" Rickie lunged forward, trying to stop JT, but two shots penetrated her svelte torso. She jerked with the impact. "NO!" Rickie yelled again, as JT fired one final shot, the muzzle flash lighting up the dark room.

Rickie fell to the floor in a dead faint.

8

THEN

"You're never going to believe what I found in Momma's jewelry box!" I grinned mischievously at Lily.

"Why were you looking through her jewelry box?" Lily asked, nonplussed.

I laughed. "Because it's *jewelry*, silly! So sparkly and pretty! What girl doesn't want to look at diamonds and rubies and emeralds? One day I'm going to have all those pretty things too!"

"Well, I hope you put it back just as it was. You know how tidy Momma is. She'll notice if anything is amiss."

"You're such a party-pooper, Lily," I said, pouting.

Lily shrugged. "I may be a party-pooper, but I am curious. What'd you find?"

"Just you wait and see," I said, opening the drawer to my bedside table and pulling out what looked like a handmade cigarette.

"Mom *smokes*?" Lily asked, eyebrows raised.

"Not cigarettes. This is marijuana."

Lily's jaw dropped in shock. "Our mom smokes *reefer*?"

"Sure looks that way. There were six of these little beauties inside a hidden drawer. I didn't think she'd notice if one was missing."

"Are you joking? It's Rosemary Reyes? *Of course* she'll notice." Lily looked thoughtful. "I wonder if Daddy knows."

"Now you're the one being stupid." I said. "Daddy wouldn't tolerate that for a second. Hell, she probably smokes them to keep her cool around him."

"True. Can you imagine being married to a man like him?" Lily shuddered.

"I can't imagine being married to *a man*," I said, sticking out my tongue.

Lily winced at her *faux pas*, then chuckled. "Yeah, there's that, I guess."

She looked at me. I looked at her. Before long, we were both rolling on the bed, laughing so hard tears streamed down our cheeks.

"Oh, my poor stomach muscles," Lily said breathlessly, hands cradling her belly.

"Who knew laughing was such a workout?" Catching my breath, I sat up, the joint cushioned in my palm. I looked at it thoughtfully and held it in front of Lily's face. "So, we gonna do this?"

Lily held up her hands. "Nope, not me. I prefer being in control of my own faculties, thank you very much."

"Fine. Didn't figure you would anyway," I said, grabbing a pack of matches and lighting up. Taking a deep drag, I found myself coughing and gagging. The feeling of a raging fire scorching the inside of my lungs was quite unpleasant.

The next drag was a little easier. As I continued smoking, the fiery feeling eased, and another took its place—a calmness washed over me. Colors became more vivid. Lily's voice was clearer, and I could smell her citrus perfume, though I hadn't been able to before.

"Ivy, you need to put that stinky thing out! Daddy will smell it when he gets home!"

"Okay," I said, happy to oblige. I was already high anyway…

I watched as Lily opened the window, then left. Or at least I thought I watched her. I plopped back against my pillow and gazed at the lovely room around me.

Relaxed. So very, very relaxed. Momma has some good stuff…

Seconds later, the door flew open, and Lily ran back inside. "He's here! Straighten up!" She grabbed a pillow and fanned it, trying to clear the stale, smoky air.

I laughed. "Don't be silly. You're such a worrywart! He isn't due for hours." My brain couldn't comprehend her ramblings.

"Ivy, it's *been* hours! You've been *stoned* for hours! Now get up!"

"Shit!"

Alarmed, I stumbled to my feet just as a giant form filled the doorway.

Daddy sniffed, then looked pointedly at the snuffed-out joint lying haphazardly on my nightstand. Lumbering across the room, he picked it up, smelled it, and asked, "Want to tell me where you obtained marijuana, Ivy?" As always, his voice was heavy with sarcasm, as if he'd rehearsed what he was going to say.

Knowing I couldn't throw Momma under the bus, but unable to come up with any names when I was still floating high, I mumbled, "I don't remember."

"Daddy, she thought it was just a cigarette. She didn't mean to…"

He looked at Lily with amusement. "Interestingly enough, Lily, I don't allow cigarettes under this roof, either."

It was probably good that I *was* stoned; otherwise, his condescending tone might've made me punch him. Especially since his smokes were the worst smelling of them all…*cigars*.

Face to face with me, he said maliciously, "Do you remember how I told you there would be serious consequences if I ever caught you drinking again? Marijuana is much worse than liquor. Now it's time to pay the piper, Ivy Reyes." He clenched his fist.

"No!" Lily jumped on his back, trying to prevent him from seriously hurting me.

"Get the fuck off!" He threw Lily off him, ignoring her cry of pain. Then, he punched me in the stomach as hard as he could, knocking the breath from my lungs.

I dropped, gasping.

Daddy jabbed his finger into my chest. My skin throbbed from the force. "You! I don't know what the fuck is wrong with you—what devil possesses your soul—but we're gonna set you on the right path today, young lady." Hot spittle flew from his mouth and hit my face. He glanced at Lily, then back at me. "I'm gonna teach your goody-goody sister a lesson today, too." As he exited the room, he pointed at each of us. "Do not move. I'll be back."

Lily sat on the floor, chin resting on her knees, quietly crying…while I tried to gulp some air into my oxygen-starved body. My diaphragm felt broken, my lungs deflated.

"I'm so sorry, Ivy," Lily said, hiccupping through her sobs. "I tried to help."

"You didn't do anything wrong." Each word was punctuated by a deep breath. "It's my fault."

A coil of rope landed with a dull thud between us.

"Come on, Lily." When she didn't move, Daddy pointed toward the white cast iron radiator. "Move it! I don't have all day!" When she was positioned, he tied her wrists to the heater. "Your job is to sit here for as long as I say, to keep an eye on your poorly behaved sister."

Then it was my turn. Forcing me to lie flat on my back in a spread-eagle position, he roughly tied my wrists and ankles to the bed posts. "And your job, you sick little bitch, is to think about what a menace you've been to our family." Just before he closed the door behind him, he added, "If you need to piss or shit, do it in your bed. You'll be there for a while."

I lay there, thinking only one thought: I'd be damned if I *ever* let a man treat me this poorly again.

9

NOW

"Rickie."

Something tapped his cheek.

"Rickie, come on, buddy. Wake up."

Rickie opened his eyes to a blurry montage. Leaking pipes illuminated by the flashlight sitting on the floor, the dead girl on the gurney, and JT's pale face looming over him. Remembering what JT had done, Rickie jerked away, frantically crab-walking backward across the floor.

"Get the fuck away from me, man!"

JT followed. "No, no, it's all right. It's okay." His voice was soothing, calm, as he sat beside Rickie, who recoiled as JT placed a reassuring hand on his raised knee. "Take it easy. Just take it easy, bro."

"Take it easy, JT?" The words spit from his mouth with a ferocity he'd never felt before. "You fucking killed her, man! You killed her with *my fucking gun!*"

"Now hold on a second—"

Rickie was nearly in tears. "You son of a bitch! You're such a sick motherfucker, JT."

"Hey, look at her!"

"You're a fucking murderer, man."

"Look…*look!*" JT pointed toward the girl.

Rickie gawked as the girl repositioned her head and lifted her leg with no obvious signs of pain. "What…?"

"She's pretty active for a dead girl, don't you think?"

"What the fuck?" Rickie said, squinting his eyes as if to verify what he was seeing was real. He glanced at JT to seek confirmation.

"I had to bring you down here, man. Had to make you see this for yourself."

"We've got to get her to a fucking hospital before she bleeds to death!"

Impatient, JT replied, "She ain't gonna bleed to death, man."

Rickie stood, slowly walking toward the gurney.

Behind him, JT said, "You had to see it for yourself, Rickie. Because I knew you wouldn't believe me if I just told you."

He studied the girl—the *Deadgirl* as JT had called her—and noticed how little blood trickled from the bullet wounds. Her body was sweat covered, bruised…*grimy as fuck*…but still very much alive. "Jesus."

JT, still sitting against the wall, nodded in agreement. "Tell me about it. I thought I was going crazy."

Rickie's eyes wouldn't…*couldn't*…leave the girl. This girl who should be dead but…wasn't. "This is some crazy shit, man."

"Yeah." JT cleared his throat. "So, uh, I wasn't telling the complete…*truth* earlier. You see, I was fucking her, like I said. Her pussy was wet, man. I started strangling her, and I heard her neck…*crack*. I felt it snap beneath my thumbs. I broke her fucking neck, man. I *know* that I did."

"No way," Rickie whispered, fixated on the dark purple, finger-shaped bruises circling her throat.

"I was trying to think what I was going to do about it, and she started moving again!" JT continued. "I thought I was going crazy. Didn't stop me from fucking her, though."

Rickie watched as Deadgirl—he hated that he was now

thinking of her in that way—looked around the room, eyes blank.

Until her gaze met his.

Somehow, through their connection, Rickie was able to see JT's attack from her perspective—his head bobbing as he thrust inside her, a greasy strand of hair falling across his forehead, his maniacal grin as he strangled her, the lust on his face as she screamed and growled, the thrusting becoming more vigorous.

The pain. And then…blackness.

Rickie gasped.

Meanwhile, unaware, JT kept up a steady stream of word vomit. "I stuck my thumbs real deep into her neck, until she quit moving."

Rickie's perspective shifted again, and he was once more looking at Deadgirl. The *victim*. He saw profound sadness in her brown eyes. Her mouth opened as if to speak, but there were no words. Rickie wasn't sure she *could* talk.

"A few minutes later, she started kicking again. I've killed her three times now." JT put a cigarette in his mouth. "But look at her." He motioned to the gurney before lighting up.

"This isn't real, man," Rickie said, as Deadgirl's eyes rolled back. "This isn't real. Is she on drugs?"

JT took a long drag. "I've never seen no drugs that will let you take three bullets like nothing happened."

"Jesus. Where do you think she came from?"

"Maybe she was a patient here?" JT shrugged. "Maybe they did some mad scientist experiment or some shit on her? Why you askin' me?"

"Who the fuck knows what they did with the leftover people…the hopeless ones," Rickie said, his voice sad. Deadgirl's eyes closed. Rickie watched her chest slowly rise and fall. "Shit, man. She can't be killed. It's a superpower! I mean, it's fucking crazy!" He ran his fingers through his hair, a small smile playing upon his lips. "It's so fucking crazy!" His breaths came in excited gasps. "It's…it's…awesome!"

"Superpowers? She look like a superhero to you? Naked Girl, or something? Maybe her super-strength and laser beam eyes are useless against those kryptonite chains."

"I'm being serious, man."

"Maybe you're right." JT nodded. "She sure as hell has the power to give me a hard-on. Pussy power?"

"Fuck you, man."

JT smirked, joining Rickie beside the gurney. He observed as Rickie timidly reached out, with a sense of fear and morbid fascination, and rubbed his fingertips gently across Deadgirl's rib cage. She jerked as he pulled his hand back.

"Man, she's so cold."

"Well, she *is* naked."

"So, what do we do with her?" Rickie asked, as Deadgirl stretched against the hard surface of the gurney.

"I've been thinking about that. She's dead, ain't no doubt about that. We tell the cops, take her to the hospital, it's gonna be a shit storm of questions we can't answer. Like what bullets from your gun are doing inside her." JT handed the gun back to Rickie.

"You're not fucking funny, man."

"I mean, we could leave her be, you know? Just forget about her, I guess. But somebody else is bound to find her eventually, right?" He stood at the foot of the bed and rubbed his forehead with the sleeve of his flannel shirt. "Or we could destroy her."

Rickie looked at him, dismayed.

JT laughed. "Aren't you supposed to get her kind in the brain pan or something?"

"'Her kind,' man? What the fuck are you saying?" Rickie sighed. "This isn't a joke, JT."

"And destroying her doesn't seem right. Look at those tits! I don't mind telling you, she's one fine fucking piece of ass, dead or not."

Disgusted, Rickie punched JT's arm. "Knock it off, bro. You a fuckin' necro now?"

"Like my momma always said, 'Don't knock it until you've tried it.' Sure, she *is* some kind of…monster, or something." For the first time, JT looked unsure. "But she's our monster." Several uncomfortable seconds passed. "So, whatcha think?"

"About what?" Rickie asked, confused.

"About hot pussy? Straight out of porn! Anytime we want it, boy. You and…" His voice cracked. "You and me, Rickie."

"You can't be serious. I'm not fucking touching her, man," Rickie said, his words tinged with anger. "It's just asking for trouble. Trouble I don't need, okay? And you can't fucking be serious. Come on."

"Yeah, I think I am serious." JT gave an embarrassed chuckle. "Come on! What else do you want to do? Take her home and introduce her to your mom, or what?"

Rickie started to walk away, then turned back. "I've got to think about this, okay?"

"Well, you take all the time you need, 'cuz…" He rattled the chains imprisoning her legs. "…she ain't going anywhere."

"This is too fucking much," Rickie said, gazing at Deadgirl.

"She's staying here."

"Okay," Rickie said, nodding slightly. "Okay. But this stays between you and me, right?"

"Yeah. You got it, buddy." JT looked quickly away.

"I'm serious, man. This is our secret. Me and you. JT and Rickie."

Ignoring him, JT asked, "Hey, you want to see something?" Without waiting for an answer, he slowly ran his hand up her leg. She immediately started shaking and groaning as he tickled her thighs near the thick patch of dark pubic hair. As his hand moved away from her core, she quieted, and her body relaxed. "Kind of fucked up, right?"

10

THEN

"I'm falling in love with you," I said, a blush coloring my cheeks.

Carrie said nothing. Just solemnly removed her clothes and stood before me, her long, wavy blonde hair draped over her shoulders. Large breasts with taupe-colored nipples begged to be licked and suckled.

During the past year, I'd had my hands on them many times, but this was the first time circumstances allowed me to actually see them. All I could think about was taking one of those perfect little nubs into my mouth. Her tiny waist blossomed into full hips and a bottom I couldn't keep my hands off. Tanned, shapely legs ended in ten adorably symmetrical toes.

Yes. I noticed things like that, and God, I cherished everything about this girl.

Unashamedly, and likely with too much puppy-like exuberance, I stripped off my clothes too. Though not as feminine or perfect as Carrie's, I knew I still had a nice body, and I was more than ready to give it to her as we consummated our relationship. I'd been waiting for this moment for so long.

I'd brought blankets and pillows into our family's winery— a cute little cobblestone-sided building which sat at the very western-edge of our acreage—along with a bottle of Cabernet Sauvignon pilfered from our wine cabinet. Everyone else was at the theater for the evening. I'd pretended to be sick, and after much debate, a lot of sweating on my part, and a few skeptical glances from Daddy, it was decided I'd be left to my own devices at home. Lily knew the real story, of course. I never kept secrets from her, but the rest of them assumed I was currently passed out in my sick bed.

"Be careful, Poison. And for Pete's sake, make sure you're back in the house long before we're expected," Lily had whispered earlier, giving me a stern look. That was quickly followed by a lopsided grin. "Have *lots* of fun." Giving me a wink, she ran to the car and climbed inside.

Hours of glorious freedom stretched before Carrie and me as our naked bodies pressed together. Her skin was smooth, soft, and warm. Taut muscles strained against mine. Wine barrels in various stages of fermentation surrounded us as we writhed and moaned, sharing sweet talk and passionate kisses.

A long while later, momentarily sated, and drinking wine in our makeshift bed, Carrie looked at me mischievously. "You're the best I've ever had, Ivy."

"Oh, yeah, and how many others have you had?"

"Lots. Hordes. So many I can't even remember!" She giggled uncomfortably before reluctantly adding, "Ivy, you do know I've been with a guy, right?"

I felt my heart drop into my stomach. Why would she wait until the first time we made love to bring this up? I thought she was a virgin. She knew I wasn't, but she'd never mentioned any other partners. It's not like there were hundreds of teenage lesbians living in the Napa Valley. My voice was stoic as I responded. "No, you've never mentioned that."

Carrie looked down at her glass of wine. "I've wanted to so badly, but I didn't know how. I know you aren't attracted to guys at all...but I am. I...I like both," she stammered.

"Who?"

This time, she blushed. "Billy."

"Billy *Small*?"

"Yeah."

"So you like guys with IQs lower than the number of inches their dick measures?"

"If it makes you feel any better, given those parameters, his IQ would be three."

"The 'Small' name is accurate, huh?"

She flashed a small, nervous grin. "He had bad breath too."

"Charming. So, it seems to me that you've been a very naughty girl, Carrie Anna Rutherford. Keeping secrets from your girlfriend, and all."

Hearing the lightheartedness in my voice, the tension in her shoulders eased. Playing along, she said, "So naughty." She sipped her wine, a glint in her eye as she ran her finger along the side of my breast. "So *very* naughty, Ivy."

"What should we do about such undignified behavior from a lovely young woman of means?"

"Punishment. I need to be punished *so good*."

I placed her wine glass on a nearby table, then pushed her gently back against the fluffy pillows. Spreading her legs, I buried my face into her musky warmth.

"That…feels…incredible." She moaned, breaths coming in short gasps, hips gyrating up and down. I took my time, feeling keen satisfaction as her body shuddered beneath mine.

Then it was my turn.

Positioning my body between her legs, I thrust my pussy against hers, grinding my clit against the delicate plateaus of her pelvic bone. Carrie responded by pushing up and rubbing herself against me. Every part of my body tingled. I gave her breast a soft squeeze, running my tongue along her neck. Hearing her moans of pleasure sent me spiraling over the edge.

Then a sinister chuckle echoed throughout the winery. "You just can't seem to stop yourself from getting into trouble, can you, Ivy?"

11

NOW

"The moment of death is a scientifically definable occurrence, marked by a lack of pupil response, an absence of reflex, and cessation of cardiac action."

Mr. Harrison, the biology teacher, droned on and on, while Rickie idly sketched in his notebook. On the same page where he'd previously drawn a headless woman whose vagina was a screaming mouth, he now worked intently on a lady whose eyes were empty, black sockets…her neck wrapped inside a noose. Droplets of black blood dribbled down her chest from three protruding nails, while dark, thorny vines growing from her dripping pussy ripped off her arms and legs.

The bell signifying the end of class rang, startling Rickie out of his daze. He looked at his artwork and grimaced.

"Remember! Your oral assignments are due this Friday!"

Oral assignments? Rickie didn't know what the hell he was even talking about.

His classmates filed quickly out of the room, but he slunk down in his seat, eyes distant as he stared out the window.

* * *

Rickie popped a potato chip into his mouth. His lunch—a dry, tasteless burger—seemed more inedible than usual as he watched JoAnn flirt with her quarterback boyfriend, Johnny. Rickie loathed the arrogant prick and never quite figured out what she saw in him. Dude even looked like a douche, with his preppy designer labels, tight, tucked in shirts that showcased his muscles, and too-short haircut. Their relationship made Rickie's stomach hurt. He flinched as she rose to her tiptoes to kiss Johnny's lips.

"Yo, Rickie! Wassup?"

Rickie gave a brief nod. "Hi, Wheeler."

Besides JT, Wheeler was Rickie's only friend. He reeked of weed. His clothes, at least two sizes too big, hung on his lanky frame. The long hair that was visible beneath the rim of his beanie was greasy, and his overall personal hygiene left a lot to be desired. But he was a nice guy. Not the brightest…but nice.

"Went home early yesterday, huh? Ya feelin' all right?"

Rickie didn't respond, still glumly watching as Johnny kissed JoAnn's neck.

"Mister Talkative today, I guess." Wheeler stole a potato chip from Rickie's plate. "What's up with you?"

"Sorry, man." He fiddled with another chip. "Just thinking."

Wheeler followed his gaze. "Thinking about JoAnn Skinner again?"

Rickie laughed ruefully, knowing he was busted.

"You better watch it, buddy. Johnny won't take kindly to you eyeing his girl."

Across the field, JoAnn and Johnny continued their make-out session.

Wheeler patted Rickie on the back as the bell rang, before stealing another chip. "Have a good one, bro."

Rickie gave Wheeler a brief, absent-minded wave, hearing JoAnn's voice. "I have to go!" She laughed as she tried to pull away.

"No," Johnny playfully replied, pulling her back toward him.

"Yes." JoAnn pushed him away, smiled flirtatiously, and walked off.

Despondent, Rickie threw his food into the trash bin and headed to class.

* * *

During the final period of the day, Rickie walked absent-mindedly through the aisles of the school library, only halting when his eyes fell on the spines of two books: one titled *The Tibetan Book of the Dead* and the other, *The Egyptian Book of the Dead*. Contemplating the possible differences—could the way humans experience death be based solely on their cultural or religious beliefs?—he didn't hear when Mr. Harrison joined him.

"Hey, Rickie. Everything all right?"

"I'm just thinking..." he replied, voice monotone, still focused on the books, "...that the dead should stay dead."

Mr. Harrison nodded knowingly. "So you're thinking about reincarnation."

Rickie remained silent.

"Some people believe in life after death," Mr. Harrison paused, contemplating his words. "You're entitled to whatever beliefs you like, Rickie. Personally, I'd like to think the dead are happy where they are. That they wouldn't want to come back, because what they earned...." He gave Rickie an arrogant grin. "...is far more glorious than this."

"Yeah," Rickie whispered, gazing at the gold-plated spines of the books. He turned. "But what do you know, Mr. Harrison? Even dying might not get you outta this fucking place."

Pushing past the stunned teacher, he left the library.

* * *

"What's up, Wheeler, man?" Rickie said, tugging Wheeler's hoodie over his head. "Hey, what you doin' today? Wanna go see if Wes has any weed?"

"Nah, man, I can't." Wheeler grinned happily. "I got plans."

"Pfft," Rickie scoffed. "What, a hot date?"

"Maybe."

The idea of Wheeler…*Wheeler*…having a date made Rickie laugh.

"Later, bro," Wheeler said, grabbing his backpack and walking away.

Trying to contain his disappointment, Rickie yelled after him, "All right. Later!"

A hot date? He shook his head, chuckling again as he made his way home.

12

THEN

Tears pummeled my cheeks as I stared out the rain-slicked window of Daddy's brand new 1945 Jaguar. Unsurprisingly, his sense of pride for his fancy ivory-colored car far outweighed his pride for his lesbian daughter. I was an embarrassment, a 'sexual deviant'...a symbol to his church buddies that he'd failed as a parent *and* a Christian.

Though I tried not to think about the events that had transpired over the past few weeks—everything that had led to this massively fucked-up moment—the images inevitably wormed their way into my brain, like nasty parasites, again and again.

That night in the winery, I was in the beginning throes of an orgasm when Daddy pulled me, by my hair, off Carrie. The sensations had started before I knew he was there, and there was nothing I could do but helplessly ride the waves. The satisfied smirk he'd been wearing as he caught me in the act was quickly replaced by disgusted rage when he realized what was happening.

He'd probably never seen a woman orgasm before. Poor Momma.

Carrie scrambled to cover herself from Daddy's gaze. Still holding me by my hair, yanking it with great force, he said,

"Well, well, well. Little Carrie Rutherford. Bet your daddy won't be thrilled to hear his pretty daughter is a lesbo bull-dyke."

Carrie, refusing to cry and maintaining her dignity despite being wrapped in a fuzzy, peach-colored blanket, said, "Seeing as my sex life is none of his business—or, frankly, none of yours, Mr. Reyes—I'd prefer you kept this to yourself." Daddy snorted and started to speak, but she cut him off. "Otherwise, I'll be forced to tell everyone in town that your wife is responsible for the Vintners Association. That you have the business sense of a jellyfish and rely on her for everything. Why, Mr. Reyes, I might even be forced to say that you'd be absolutely nothing without that wife of yours. Everybody in town already knows it's true, but hearing me say it, knowing your daughter is my best friend…" She looked at me with a small smile. "…well, I suspect that would lend some credence to my words."

Daddy's expression was deadly. "Are you threatening me?" His voice was a soft hiss. A cobra waiting to strike.

"Of course I am. I have nothing to lose. In fact, I'll do it again. If you don't let go of Ivy's hair this instant, I'll walk home right now and call the county sheriff, my dear old Uncle John, and tell him you get great enjoyment from physically assaulting your very petite teenage daughter."

Roaring with anger, Daddy shoved me toward Carrie, causing us both to collapse onto the unyielding wooden floor. "Get out of my winery, you little bitch. And stay off my land! If I ever see you back here again, I'll tell everyone what a degenerate pervert you really are!"

Not wasting a second, we grabbed our clothes and raced from the winery into the long rows of the vineyard. When we were far enough away that I knew Daddy couldn't see us in the dark, we stopped and dressed. The silence between us was unbearable.

Finally, I couldn't stand it anymore. "Carrie, I…I don't even know where to begin. They weren't due home until midnight.

It's like, what? Nine-thirty? I don't know what happened. I'm so sorry."

"It's okay." She ran her hand gently down the side of my face. "I don't think he's going to tell my parents."

"He'd have to be dumb as a bag of rocks to do so after your little speech," I said. We both giggled nervously. "Where did that come from, anyway?"

She looked away. "Everyone knows what your dad is like, Ivy. He's a narcissist bully with an inferiority complex. He demeans others to make himself feel better. What makes him an even scarier creature is that he's smart enough to know he's not smart at all, so he feels he must squash everyone around him to continue to feel in control."

"And he's a sexist pig," I chimed in.

"That too," Carrie chuckled, but quickly sobered up. "I'm sorry I made this even more complicated for you. I don't want him to take his anger at me out on you. Or Lily."

"We're used to it." I shrugged, ashamed.

"Why don't you stay at my house tonight? My parents won't object, and it will ease my mind. I need to know you're safe."

The offer was tempting, but I knew it would ultimately make things even worse for me…if that were possible.

I ruefully shook my head. "I can't."

She exhaled a long, weary sigh. "I know."

We gazed at the twinkling lights in the distance, holding hands, not knowing if it would be the last time.

Sadly…it was.

13

NOW

Rickie let his bike drop unceremoniously to the ground beside the steps leading to the back door. The tires spun lazily as he went inside. Going straight to the kitchen, he poured himself a glass of orange juice, then eyed the vodka in the freezer.

"Ma, Clint…you home?" When he didn't get an answer, he pulled the vodka from the freezer and liberally laced his drink.

Carrying it to his bedroom, the caramel-colored walls decorated with band posters and his twisted sketches, he took off his jacket and sat on the edge of the bed. The icy liquid felt good sliding down his parched throat. After a second long swallow, he set the glass on the floor and nestled into the unmade bed.

Hands behind his head, he watched the shadows shifting on the ceiling and felt his body relax.

The afternoon sun filtering through green leaves gently blowing in the breeze. Long, auburn hair glistening in the sunlight. JoAnn's smiling face, her gaze happy and flirtatious, light brown freckles stippled across her nose and cheeks, dark eyelashes a stark contrast against her porcelain skin. Turning away, she glances back over her shoulder. A half-smile, showcasing perfect teeth.

Rickie's hand slid beneath the waistband of his jeans.

The sunlight is brighter now, the leaves harder to distinguish. JoAnn smiles and bites her lip seductively. She's between his legs. Her hair is parted in the center, lips shiny with gloss. The look on her face is alluring, titillating. A look that says, "I know how to make your dreams come true, and I will." Her head moves rhythmically up and down, up and down.

His breaths became heavier as his hand moved faster.

JoAnn stops and looks at him, her green eyes piercing. Her image fades and another takes its place. Bloodshot brown eyes stare defiantly at him, an unhealthy purple hue coloring the skin beneath them. Despite the stringy hair and pallid complexion, the girl is still a knockout. Her expression is complacent…until she lunges forward, teeth snapping.

He jerked, hand no longer inside his pants, and moaned in his sleep.

The images continuously shift…
JoAnn looking seductive.
Deadgirl slowly turning her head.
JoAnn readying herself to suck his cock.
Deadgirl wearing a sinister, knowing smirk.
Deadgirl smiling, Deadgirl snarling, Deadgirl snapping her teeth,
Deadgirl smirking, Deadgirl biting…

14

THEN

We'd been driving for hours. I passed the time watching the ever-changing scenery. A cloud of sadness enveloped me as the lush greens of the wine country—the only place I'd ever known—faded to the harsh browns of the southern California desert.

Daddy hummed quietly to himself, giving me the occasional smug glance in the rearview mirror. Momma nervously twisted a tissue inside her hands, shredding it, but saying nothing. When she looked at me, it was only to offer an encouraging smile. Then she'd face forward, and I'd hear sniffling as she fought to control her tears.

Many times throughout the days leading to this trip, I'd heard my parents arguing in their bedroom.

"This is nonsense, Edgar. She doesn't belong there!"

"The hell she doesn't!"

"She's a young girl finding her way."

"She's a goddamn pervert! We need to get her the hell away from Lily and Violet!"

Daddy always won.

My memories drifted to that day…

I'd left Carrie after an excruciating goodbye and walked

slowly back to my house, blind panic erupting inside my chest. I wasn't embarrassed. Humans were sexual beings, and I was doing what humans do. The problem was, according to Daddy, I was doing it with the wrong gender.

I was forced to stop every few minutes to catch my breath as the anxiety became intolerable. I had no idea what to expect, given the extreme circumstances, but when I reached our yard, I could only stop and gape.

For once, Daddy had managed to shock me. I'd expected shouting and slaps and punches. Instead, the house was dark, silent. Not a single light shone from within. Even the light illuminating the front door, which was always kept on at night, was shut off...Daddy's not-so-subtle way of telling me I was unwelcome.

I tried the knob, just in case. Unsurprisingly, it was locked, and the spare key was no longer in its hiding spot beneath the planter. Racing around the side of the house, I glanced at our second-story bedroom window, praying it was open. It wasn't. The lavender gingham curtains were pulled tightly against the night.

Not even Lily could fix the mess I'd created.

Letting out a pent-up breath, I plopped onto the ground, leaning against the trusty tree I'd used dozens of times to sneak in and out of the house. Tonight, though, was *not* the night to be sneaky. Daddy probably had a bear trap below the window that I'd step in if I dared to try and get inside.

"All right, Ivy, what to do, what to do?" I mumbled, looking at the surrounding area for inspiration.

My eyes caught a glimpse of something white hidden within the shadows near the house. I crouched to get a better look and realized it was a folded sheet of paper. Given its proximity to our window, I suspected it was a message from Lily.

Moving to a section of yard bathed in moonlight, I read her words:

Oh, Poison…what happened?

I've never seen Daddy like he was tonight. He refused to talk, just went around breaking things. Momma was helpless to stop him. She kept asking where you were, but he wouldn't answer. The only thing he said was, "Lock down the house immediately." Violet and Robert— little shits—loved every minute of the drama. Big surprise. Sometimes I wonder how we're related to such awful people.

Daddy forced me to lock our bedroom window. I'm so sorry. I hope you can find a warm place to sleep. Honestly, if it were me, I'd stay away tomorrow, too. Maybe Carrie would let you stay with her? Daddy needs time to cool off. Given the way he was acting, I'm scared what he'd do if he saw you right now.

Keep checking beneath our window. I'll drop messages when I can.

Love you.

I couldn't show up unexpectedly at Carrie's house. I'd caused her enough problems. The winery was out. My memories there were still too fresh and raw. Daddy probably had a padlock on the door now anyway. Though it was late-October in California, the nighttime temperatures in the valley dropped routinely into the forties. My outfit consisted of a pleated skirt, a short-sleeved cardigan, and a pair of peep-toe slingbacks…not exactly ideal for roughing it outdoors.

Which left the storage shed.

Sitting several dozen yards behind the house, the little ramshackle building held tools, a lawnmower, bins full of old toys, and leftover cans of paint. I'd been petrified to go inside as a kid. It reminded me of a cellar…dark, shadowy, and musty.

I remember wondering how many people Daddy had buried beneath the dirt floor. Hopefully, I wasn't next.

A puff of stale air greeted me as the door creaked open. Sifting through the tubs of junk, I found a stain-covered tarp, a cotton car cover, and an old stuffed animal plush that once belonged to Robert. Placing the tarp on the floor, I nestled in, using the toy as a pillow and the car cover as a blanket. The adrenaline that had been coursing steadily through my body since Daddy showed up, crashed. Within seconds, I was asleep.

15

NOW

Agitated after the dream—or whatever the hell that bullshit was—Rickie knew he had to do something to help Deadgirl.

Putting on his jacket, he ran out of the house, hopped on his bike, and pedaled furiously across town. Spying some overgrown shrubs lining the stone wall of the nuthouse, and not wanting anyone, especially JT, to know he was there, he stashed his bike behind them. Then he slipped effortlessly through the window JT had broken the day before.

Retracing his steps, he made the long trek to the sub-basement, eventually coming face-to-face with the steel door. Heart in his throat, he looked behind him, contemplating his sanity. The place was creepy as fuck, and he owed nothing to Deadgirl. He wasn't entirely sure she was even fucking human! He also knew he couldn't live with himself if he did nothing, so he pushed his fears aside and resolutely reached for the door.

As it slowly creaked open, the first thing he heard was rattling chains. The second...grunts. Pushing through the plastic sheeting, he saw the gurney that held Deadgirl's body rocking. A lantern sitting on the floor beside the bed, illuminated what was happening.

"Fucking...*Wheeler?*"

Wheeler didn't stop thrusting as he fucked Deadgirl. "Rickie!" he yelled, breathless from his exertions and grinning ear to ear. "Told ya I had a hot date!"

Deadgirl's body had been pulled down the gurney. Her legs were hanging over the edge, allowing for easier access. Though she was completely nude, Wheeler was fucking her with his pants around his ankles, boxer shorts still in place. Rickie idly wondered if he knew his ass crack was showing.

"Hey, Rickie!" JT said from the corner.

"JT, man, remember our fucking conversation?" Cigarette smoke billowed between them as Rickie got in his face. "Or did all the gas-huffing give you selective memory?"

"What's your problem, man?"

"My problem is we agreed not to tell anyone about this! What were you fucking thinking?"

"I know we did," JT said, his voice whiny. "But I didn't want to be alone, you know what I mean? I just wanted some company. And since you're too fucking squeamish to put it to this hot little fuck toy, I figured I might as well share her with somebody who doesn't mind a nice piece now and again."

"I'm here, aren't I?" Rickie shrugged his shoulders. "I mean, I'm here. And she's *not* a fuck toy."

"Well, then go get some for once instead of wishing you could, man. And what the fuck is she then? She ain't a real human being, that's for sure."

Rickie took several deep breaths to control his anger. JT turned toward Wheeler, taking a drag of his cigarette as he watched.

Deadgirl didn't make a sound.

"Dude, come on," Rickie said. "It's not like that, okay? Look. Last night, man…well. Last night she, uh…fuck! She been looking at you?"

JT pulled the cigarette from between his lips. "*What?*"

"Like she knows something?" Rickie was almost whispering.

They both paused as Wheeler groaned loudly and zipped up, a euphoric grin lighting his face.

Returning his attention to Rickie, JT laughed. "What the fuck are you talking about, Rickie? Look, we can make things easier. We can even call her JoAnn if you want."

Rickie recoiled as if he'd been slapped.

JT continued. "You know that ain't a real person, man. Right? You know that."

Rickie sighed.

"It's all right. It's okay," JT said, placating him.

"That's beside the point, man."

"Oh, is it? Well, what were you doing down here, huh?" JT was smug.

Seconds passed as Rickie tried to find the right words. He finally landed on, "I don't know, man."

"Yeah, that's what I thought."

Exasperated, Rickie said, "I'm not…that's not what…"

JT pointed at him, clicking his tongue as though Rickie had been naughty.

"Goddammit, JT!"

Wheeler, eager like a puppy, said, "If you want, man, we can, like…" He motioned with his hands. "…flip her over. We haven't hit her backside yet."

"Not a fucking chance." Rickie said.

"Rickie," JT chided, standing with his hands on his hips. "Pal. *What's wrong?*"

"This whole thing is fucking over, you guys."

JT rolled his eyes.

"Seriously," Rickie continued. "We're going to get arrested. Or worse! I mean…"

"How long have we known Wheeler?" JT replied, cutting him off. "All our lives? He knows how to keep a secret. He knows a good thing when he sees it. Don't you, Wheeler?"

"I know a good thing when I *fuck* it." Lacing his shoes, he grinned at Rickie.

"There you go," JT said. "So, you see, there's nothing to worry about, Rickie. It's just you and me and Wheeler and the…Deadgirl."

"She's not just some dead girl, man."

JT chuckled. "Well, I did kill her three times." He ruffled Rickie's hair. "Go on. Give it a try. Get on it, man."

"Man, it's fucking sweeeeeet!" Wheeler said. "You've gotta fucking get in there!"

"Go on. Go on!" JT chimed in.

Fed up, Rickie turned and walked out the door.

"Aw, Rickie. Well, all right then. Maybe come back in a couple hours?" JT raised his syrupy voice so it could be heard in the hallway. "We'll be gone! You can have a nice, private, romantic time and do lots of nice…*sensitive* things! All right then, God bless!"

Rickie didn't look back.

16

THEN

"Wake up. Wake up, goddammit!"

I opened my eyes, not knowing where I was or who was yelling at me. The sun was directly behind the bulky form, preventing me, in my disoriented state, from seeing anything. Nothing was distinguishable.

A kick to the ribs told me exactly who it was. Memories of the previous night flooded my brain, and I sat up. Crying out in pain, the abused muscles already tender and sore, I leaned against the wall.

"Your mother and I would like to speak to you. Meet us in the sitting room in ten minutes."

Heart racing, I jumped up, ran to the well, and pumped water into the tin bucket that hung on the side. Slurping the clean, cold liquid greedily from my cupped hands, I used the leftovers to splash my face. Looking around the grounds of the vineyard and seeing no one, I hiked up my skirt and used the hem to blot away the moisture, then squatted and peed on the ground. Bracing my injured ribs, I walked stiffly to the house, overcome with anxiety.

It was silent inside. Too silent.

Momma sat in a rocking chair by the window, her chair

creaking softly with each movement. Daddy stood beside the fireplace, studying the mantel. He probably thought the pose made him look powerful, or some pathetic bullshit. There was no sign of my siblings.

"Good morning," I said, timidly.

Momma offered a small smile, immediately making me feel at ease. "Morning, baby."

As if sensing he was losing his intimidation factor, my father said, "That's enough, Rosie." He looked at me. "Your brother and sisters are visiting your grandparents for the next few days. That allows us the time we need to prepare for your future." He paused, almost theatrically. The hush felt loaded, ready to destroy me. "Two weeks from today, you'll be admitted to a... *hospital*..." He couldn't hide his smirk. "...outside Los Angeles. There, you will go through various therapies, counseling, and psychoanalysis."

"But...but..." I could barely find words. "...there is *nothing* wrong with me!"

Pretending to be a caring father, the only way he knew how to parent, Daddy put his hand on my shoulder. "Homosexuality is a disease. An illness. If you want to have a normal life, Ivy, you need to be cured now, while you're still young. This is for the best."

I turned to Momma, tears hot and heavy on my flushed cheeks. "Please, don't make me do this, Momma. *Please*. You can convince Daddy this is a bad idea, right?"

She wouldn't look at me, just nervously rocked back and forth in that fucking heirloom chair.

"That's enough, Ivy." Daddy's voice was stern. "Leave your momma alone. Like me, she wants what's best for you."

"You don't give a damn about me! You never have. Don't start pretending to be father-of-the-year when everyone knows you're the saddest sack of shit in the Napa Valley!"

"Oh, Ivy, no," Momma wailed.

That was when Daddy broke my arm.

17

NOW

A feminine hand protruded from the dumpster sitting adjacent to the junkyard.

After everything that had happened over the past twenty-four hours, Rickie was completely skeeved out, but unwilling to ignore somebody in need. He kept failing Deadgirl. He sure as hell wasn't going to fail anyone else.

Upon closer inspection, he quickly realized the waxy, poreless skin wasn't real. It was a mannequin's arm poking out of the debris. Smiling in relief, Rickie continued on his way. From the corner of his eye, he saw the rubble shift. Yelping, he almost fell off his bike as a little old man climbed from the confines of the dumpster. A mannequin head was in one hand, a beer can in the other.

How in the hell was he drinking beer under all that…stuff?

The old man gave Rickie a jovial wave, then peered drunkenly at the head and slurred, "It is not in the stars to hold our destiny but in ourselves."

As he made for the junkyard entrance, Rickie thought about the man's words. He assumed it was Shakespeare or Dickens or some other old-dead-white-guy-shit, but whatever it was, he sure as fuck related.

* * *

"Whoa, whoa, whoa, whoa!" A heavyset guy wearing a greasy shirt with an embroidered nametag, came out of the junkyard's office. He had a thick beard and a permed mullet. "Look, I told you fuckers if you want weed, you need to…"

Ricky interrupted. "I need some bolt cutters, Wes."

Wes paused, perplexed by the unexpected request. "Got any money?"

"Come on." Rickie sighed. "You know I'm good for it, man."

Wes looked pointedly at his bike and said nothing.

Rickie stifled a sigh. *Fuck.*

* * *

It was dark by the time Rickie made it back to the nuthouse on foot. He crept silently through the hallways, listening closely for JT and Wheeler, but heard nothing. Inching toward the closed door, he placed his ear gently against the cold metal. Confident he was alone—at least for the moment—he made his way into the room. The floor was covered with beer cans and fast-food wrappers.

As he turned the corner, he saw her, shapely buttocks highlighted in the dim lighting. She'd been flipped onto her stomach. Rickie refused to think about what those assholes had done to her.

Sensing him there, she slowly shifted her body, rattling the heavy chains. Her head was turned awkwardly to the right. She moaned against the bloody gag in her mouth.

He listened once again for sounds inside the building. Hearing nothing, he crouched so he and Deadgirl were face-to-face. "Everything's going to be okay, all right? I'm going to get you out of here."

She studied him, eyes unblinking. Rickie saw something in

that gaze. Something real. Something heartfelt. Something…human.

"I'm here to help you, okay?"

A loud clang echoed through the building.

"Shit!" Rickie jumped and faced the door, his hand gripping the gurney. When seconds passed without further incident, he allowed himself to relax.

Something tickled his hand.

Startled, he watched as Deadgirl's finger gently stroked his. The nails were yellowed and splintered, grimy with dirt. Her gaze was devoid of emotion. Almost timidly, she covered his hand with hers.

Stunned, he asked, "Do you understand me? Because I'm going to get you out of here. But you have to be quiet, okay? You *have* to be quiet." Tenderly removing the gag from her mouth, he said, "I'm sorry. I'm so sorry."

Her eyes rolled back.

"Okay," Rickie said, trying to convince himself he was doing the right thing.

Pulling the bolt cutters from his backpack, he inspected the chains from top to bottom, and noticed a small tattoo hidden below her right wrist restraint. It was tiny, delicate, faded… some sort of plant or greenery.

"How did you get this? When?"

This time, when she looked at him, he swore he saw a tear. That was all he needed.

He cut the first chain.

18

THEN

"Do you trust me?" Lily asked, wrapping her hair around her finger, attempting a look of innocence.

It was the day before I was scheduled to leave, and I was clumsily packing the last of the approved clothing into my suitcase. Doing anything with a bulky cast on your dominant arm was tiresome and frustrating.

The hospital was very specific about what I could and couldn't bring. Leaving behind all my pretty clothes made me sad, but Lily promised to keep them safe for me. The rest of my belongings had been boxed up and taken to the local Goodwill, but not before Violet and Robert claimed what they wanted. It felt like my family had already killed me off.

"When you're healed and back home, you'll be able to find a job, earn your own money, and buy anything your heart desires," Daddy had told me, enjoying his power over me far too much.

"You know I trust you," I told Lily, sneaking my diary and pen into a small, hidden pocket.

"Then come with me." She looked mischievous. "Right now!"

I was depressed. It was hard to garner enthusiasm for

anything. "I really need to finish packing." My voice was tired, unenthusiastic.

"Come on, Poison! This is special. I promise you'll love it." She looked so excited, I couldn't tell her no.

Daddy and Momma were at the winery inventorying the barrels of wine. Violet was visiting a friend, and Robert was… somewhere…doing *stinky boy* things. We slipped out of the house unobserved and walked hand-in-hand down the road to the home of our nearest neighbor.

Lily knocked on the front door. It was opened by a man in his mid-twenties. He had long, flowing, shoulder-length hair and a goatee. Short, military-type cuts and clean-shaven faces were the norm. I liked that he wasn't afraid to be different…that he bucked against the system. If I weren't a lesbian…

Apparently, Lily felt the same, minus the lesbian bit. "Hi, Charley. How's it going?" The blush tingeing her cheeks was the cutest thing I'd seen in weeks.

"Hey, Lily. Great to see you again! Things are going well here at the old Rothchild homestead." His gaze lingered on her a little longer than necessary before he looked at me. "And you must be Ivy."

"The one and only," I said, self-consciously. I had no idea what this guy knew about my situation.

"It's nice to finally meet you. Lily talks about you all the time." He motioned us inside. "Please, both of you, come in. I've got everything set up in the art room, so just head on back."

Lily led the way.

Amused, I whispered covertly to her. "And just how do you know where his art room is?"

She avoided my knowing glance. "Daddy hates him. Calls him a 'worthless no-good varmint.' Obviously, I made sure to befriend him. If he's not good enough for Daddy, he's plenty good enough for me."

I laughed. "He seems like a good friend to have," I said, feeling the weight on my shoulders lessen.

Lily would be okay. She had friends, goals, possibly a new romance...*a life*. Knowing this made me more receptive to whatever it was she had planned.

We entered a room that reeked of turpentine but looked like the inside of a rainbow. Colors...gorgeous, bright, saturated colors everywhere! Canvases hung on walls, sat on easels, and were stacked against every available surface.

"This is amazing," I said, my eyes flittering between the paintings.

"I know," Lily said, her voice dreamy. "He's beyond talented."

Charley entered carrying three glasses of lemonade on a tray. "Here we go, ladies. Help yourselves. Let's get a little sugar into your systems before we get started. Don't want you passing out on me."

"Uh...what?" I looked at Lily. "I'll be passing out...*why*?"

"Tattoos!" Lily said. "We're getting wrist tattoos. You'll get an ivy vine, I'll get a lily, and they'll be ours. Nobody else has to know."

I loved the idea, but...

"What about Daddy? If he finds out his *daughters* have tattoos..."

"We're going to hide yours under your cast, and Charley got me a bracelet to wear that will hide mine." She smiled. "It'll be fine."

That's all I needed to hear. Impulsive was my middle name. "Let's do it!"

Several hours later, I had a delicate ivy vine that wrapped entirely around my right wrist. Charley used techniques that created multiple shades of green, and the leaves absolutely popped off my skin with vibrant color. Then he used Papier-mâché to extend the cast just enough to hide my beautiful tattoo. I was giddy.

The flower on Lily's wrist was lovely. Bright, vivid orange petals with traces of pink near the center. Green leaves and white baby's breath surrounding the bloom. After he finished, Charley gave her a silver cuff bracelet, which she bashfully slid on.

"What if Daddy asks about it?"

"I'll just tell him it was yours, and I'm wearing it to feel closer to you."

I nodded, suddenly despondent. This was my last day at the only home I'd ever known. I had no idea what awaited me in Los Angeles, or when I'd see Lily again.

Before we left, I saw Charley sneak a quick peck on Lily's cheek. It made me smile.

* * *

Dinner was a quiet affair. Daddy drank more than usual but said very little.

Even Violet and Robert seemed morose. I had to wonder if it would ever occur to them that if Daddy could do this to me, he could also do it to them.

Momma, bless her, tried to create a pleasant evening. She made my favorite meal: potato soup with homemade brown bread and molasses cookies for dessert. She even wrapped some of the sweets in wax paper and tucked them into my suitcase before bed.

The truth was, though, I needed the goodbyes to end. The past two weeks had been painful. I needed to move forward, do what was required to be released, then go on with my life. Deep inside, I knew nothing would ever be the same. This was the last time I'd see my family as they were at this moment in time. Looking at all of them, my family of misfits, I captured a snapshot in my mind.

That night, I held Lily extra close.

19

NOW

Nearby yelling and whooping distracted Rickie from his task. He stood frozen, listening. "Fuck!" he whispered, realizing JT and Wheeler were still in the building.

As if sensing his distress, the girl used her newly freed hand to grab his wrist. Rickie gasped in surprise, struggling to pull himself from her iron grip, and dropping the bolt cutters in the process. Bracing his foot against the bed, he pulled as hard as he could, furiously pounding her wrist to try and break the inhumanly strong grasp. Her nails sunk deeper into his skin. Grimacing in pain and desperate to get loose, knowing he must hide before they found him, Rickie forcibly pulled his arm through her fingernail clamp. Deep, meaty gouges colored his flesh, and he fell to the ground, landing hard on his ass as he cradled the bloodied arm.

Giddy laughter and pounding footsteps sounded very close...JT and Wheeler returning from another vandalization spree. Grabbing his backpack and accidentally kicking the bolt cutters beneath the gurney as he raced for safety, Rickie dove into a dark alcove just outside the door.

"Did you leave the fucking door open, Wheeler?" JT

stopped mere feet away from Rickie's hiding place. If he turned his head…

"No, I don't think so."

"I told you to keep the door shut, didn't I?" JT's voice was sharp, his irritation evident.

Wheeler shrugged. "Why does it matter?"

Reveling in his power rush, JT replied, "I don't want anyone else messing with her. The next time I find that door left open, I will kick your ass."

Wheeler rolled his eyes and followed JT into the room, making sure to firmly shut the door behind them.

Peering through a hole in the drywall, Rickie watched JT strut toward the table.

"What's up, baby? How you doing?" He motioned Wheeler away. "Why don't you busy yourself somewhere else?"

Wheeler obligingly moved to the other side of the room.

Standing at the foot of the bed, JT studied the girl's nude body—a lion preparing to pounce. "Hey, baby, you miss me?" His hand slid over the bulge in his jeans.

Rickie was sick to his stomach. He didn't understand how JT could look at her and get turned on. All Rickie saw was a girl overwhelmed by sadness, isolation…vulnerability.

JT positioned himself between her spread legs. Smiling in anticipation, he pushed down his pants and scooted closer. The smile faded when he saw the gag was no longer in her mouth, and it morphed into pure horror when he realized her hand was free. She looked at him from the corner of her eye, her expression animalistic.

"Oh, shit!" He tried to climb off but didn't make it.

Letting out a furious growl, she swung her arm, leaving deep, razor-like furrows across his cheek. JT yelped and fell to the floor, as the girl screamed and thrashed trying to get free. On her knees, she whipped the chains, shrieking like a banshee.

Wheeler rushed over and helped JT try to restrain her.

"Fuck!" JT yelled as she landed a punch to his face. "Grab her fucking hand, man!" Wheeler struggled to maintain his grasp as she ferociously fought him. "Goddammit, get her fucking hand!"

Crushed, Rickie closed his eyes. He'd caused this.

"Fucking get her off me!" Wheeler begged, as she clawed at his skin and tried to bite him. "You ain't no help, man!"

JT shoved her from behind. Forcing her to her stomach, he screamed, "Get the fuck down!"

She continued thrashing, head pumping up and down, teeth gnashing.

"Fucking stop it!" Grabbing a length of rope, JT quickly tied her down. The girl struggled, her growls like a wounded animal.

"She could have fucking killed us, man!" Wheeler was nearly in tears.

JT spit blood onto the ground. He tried to assess the damage to his cheek by lightly touching the gouges. "Ahhhh!" He flinched in pain. "Fuck!"

"I oughta fucking bite *you*!" Wheeler yelled angrily at the girl, as she continued struggling and grunting. "How the fuck did she get free, man?"

Rickie, realizing they'd soon find the bolt cutters, eased from his hiding spot. He made it several feet before bumping into an old-fashioned infant incubator. It rammed into the wall, making a loud thud. He froze.

"Did you hear that?" JT asked. "Rickie, that you?"

Rickie ran as far as he could. Turning a corner, he stopped and braced against a wall so JT wouldn't hear his footsteps.

"*Rickie!*" Pissed, JT raced into the hallway. "If I find out it was you trying to let her loose, you're gonna regret it!"

Realizing JT's voice wasn't getting closer, Rickie exhaled and tried to catch his breath. In a glimmer of moonlight, he noticed a tiny, vine-like plant that had had sprouted through a crack in the cement.

It kinda looked like...ivy. After gazing at it for a few seconds, Rickie silently headed toward the exit.

"Might as well come out now!" JT wasn't giving up.

* * *

Wheeler, having found the bolt cutters and realizing Rickie had simply been trying to help the girl, made a split decision. JT was acting so crazy lately, he worried what he'd do if he had proof Rickie had betrayed him.

Hiding the bolt cutters beneath some trash in the corner of the room, he listened as JT continued his batshit screaming.

"Never thought you were such a goddamn sissy, Rickie! Momma's little baby. You still suckle at her tit?" He kicked the incubator. "I know it was you, man! I won't forget this!"

JT deflated. Walking back into the room, he gave Wheeler a lopsided grin. "Fuckin' A, man. If it ain't one thing, it's another."

20

THEN

We'd been driving for six hours when Daddy suddenly turned and said, "Almost there!"

Dread filled my chest. The rain had stopped, and the late afternoon sun shone through crazy looking branchless trees with giant green fronds at the top.

The city was bustling. More cars than I'd ever seen lined the streets. Military men still in uniform were everywhere, pretty women on their arms. I craned my neck looking at Warner Brothers studio as we drove past. The energy was mellow, relaxed…these people didn't seem to have a care in the world.

The longer we drove, the seedier the city became. Momma noticed it, too. "Is this the right way?" she asked nervously, fanning her face to quell her anxiety.

"Yes, dear." Daddy's voice was monotone. I could tell he was annoyed she'd had the gall to question him.

Then, we passed a sign: *Welcome to Evansburgh, California – A Nice Slice of Paradise.*

From what I could tell, it was the *opposite* of paradise… crumbling houses, trash-lined streets, mangy animals searching for food.

Daddy turned left onto a dirt road that wound through

desert scrub. After a mile, a giant, white, L-shaped, five-story building with peeling paint, rusted fixtures, and creeping vines came into view.

And there it was. My new home. The Linda Vista Lunatic Asylum.

21

NOW

Rickie sat on a bench inside the locker room, head in his hands, exhausted.

The walk home had been long last night, and it had hurt like fuck when he'd cleaned and disinfected the wounds on his arm. He'd tossed and turned once he'd finally crawled into bed.

He heard somebody enter the locker room but didn't move. The patter of footsteps headed his way, then stopped. Whoever it was took a deep breath and let it out.

Annoyed, Rickie finally looked up. A heavy-set kid with curly, dark-blonde hair, a sleeveless maroon t-shirt, and a scattering of acne on his arms and shoulders gave him a timid grin.

"Sorry!" the kid said nervously. Rickie thought his name was Walter.

He stood there, not saying anything else.

"What, man?" Rickie said, growling out the words.

The kid jumped and swallowed. "Uh, you're friends with Wheeler. You know where I could find him?"

Rickie rubbed his forehead and headed toward the door. "No."

"Because he said if I brought him ten bucks, he'd show me something."

Rickie slowly turned around. "What?" His voice was menacing.

Oblivious, the guy kept talking. "Wheeler? He said…"

Rickie pushed Walter into the lockers, his bandaged forearm tight against his throat. "Wheeler's a fucking half-wit, you dumb ass!"

The kid looked petrified.

Backing away, Rickie murmured, "He's just trying to steal your money, man." Shaking his head, he left the locker room.

* * *

Sitting side by side, JoAnn and Johnny utilized two computers in the library. JoAnn was intensely focused on her screen, seemingly trying to get some work done, but Johnny wasn't having it. Snorting with laughter, he kept turning his screen to show her what he was watching. She smiled politely but didn't interact.

"C'mon, baby. Lighten up!"

"I have an assignment I need to finish before next period."

Rickie watched them from behind a bookshelf, a Romeo pining for his Juliet. When he saw Wheeler an aisle over, JoAnn was forgotten. He ran to catch up.

"Hey, asshole!" he whispered. "Fuckin' Walter just came up to me, man…"

Interrupting, Wheeler asked, "Was it you last night?"

"Yeah, so what?"

* * *

From across the room, Johnny watched them with interest.

"What's up, Johnny-boy?" Dwyer, his best friend, asked.

Johnny shushed him, trying to hear what Rickie and Wheeler were saying.

* * *

"I'm sorry you got hurt, but…fuck!" Distracted, Rickie glanced back at JoAnn, but she was gone. It was just Johnny and his goon, Dwyer, who'd taken her seat. He was taller and thinner than Johnny, but just as douchey.

"You know what? Fuck you, Rickie! You're just fucking lucky I didn't tell JT about the bolt cutters." Wheeler turned away.

Grabbing his arm and pulling him back, Rickie said, "Yeah? Hey, why the fuck didn't you then, huh?"

* * *

"See those dipshits over there?" Johnny pointed.

Dwyer was amused. "Lots of dipshits over there. Which ones you talking about?"

"The fucking stoner and his perverted buddy. The one with the stupid, floppy hair and the big hound dog eyes. He's been looking over here all goddamn period."

"He was eyeballing JoAnn, dude," Dwyer said, smothering a laugh, not taking his eyes off the monitor. "Has been for the past two years."

"You fucking serious?"

"All them dipshits want to stick it to your squeeze, man."

"Shut the fuck up, Dwyer."

Holding up his hands, Dwyer said, "Hey man, take it easy. I'm not the one wanting to pound the shit outta JoAnn's hotbox. You got a problem with it, take it up with them."

Johnny glared at the loser, who was deep in conversation with the other idiot. "Fuckin' faggot," he muttered.

* * *

"You know what, man? Me and JT are fine," Wheeler said. "Okay, it's *you* that he's fucking worried about."

Rolling his eyes, Rickie said, "JT hasn't been to school in days, man. Somebody is going to notice, and then what?"

"What?" Wheeler asked, confused.

"They'll go looking, you fucking moron!"

"That's bullshit, man. Nobody gives a fucking shit about JT, except for JT. Not the school, certainly not his fucking grandmother, who's half-dead anyway, okay? Nobody gives a shit where he goes, or what he does. Nobody but us."

Rickie knew he was right. Defeated, he leaned against the bookshelf, saying nothing as Wheeler walked away.

22

THEN

"This can't be right!" Momma said, her expression horrified as she regarded the crumbling building. "It says it's for lunatics! Our Ivy isn't a lunatic! We can't leave her here, Edgar!"

"We can, and we will," Daddy said, stepping out of the car. "She's sick, and this *hospital*…" He emphasized the word. "…has the best cure rate for sexual deviance."

We gathered my meager belongings and headed toward the entrance. My legs were shaking so badly, I tripped over a chunk of rubble and bloodied my knees.

Momma, desperate to do something, *anything* for me, wet her handkerchief with saliva and cleaned the abrasions. "There you go, sweetheart!" Her tone was artificially cheerful. "All better! I bet they'll give you some antiseptic inside. It's a… hospital…after all," she said, craning her neck to look up at the imposing building.

"I'll be fine." I gave her a reassuring smile.

Daddy pulled open the ivory and brown iron door and waited impatiently for us to enter. I looked at everything around me—the sky, the trees, the cars, the tiny chipmunk sitting in the grass—taking it all in. I didn't know if an asylum allowed their patients to participate in outdoor activities. Taking a final deep breath of the fresh, cool air, I followed Momma inside.

A frumpy woman with a yellow stain on her white blouse sat at the front desk.

"We're checking my daughter in," Daddy said imperiously.

"Name." The woman, whose name tag read *Mary*, wasn't impressed.

"Ivy Elizabeth Reyes," I jumped in, watching her scribble my name into the register.

"Age."

"I'll be seventeen on December 31st."

Her writing was practically illegible.

The woman pulled a brown folder from a drawer. I could see my name on the tab. "Say your goodbyes. Your parents can't go any farther into the building." She crossed her arms over her ample bosom.

"Ma'am," Momma said, smiling politely at Mary. "My daughter fell outside and skinned her knees. Can you make sure the wounds get disinfected?"

Letting out an agitated breath, the grumpy, old bitch—I refused to think of her as Mary—said, "Yeah. Sure. We'll get right on that."

A scream echoed from behind the door.

"Uh...much obliged." Momma pulled me into the warmth and safety of her arms. She smelled fresh and clean, like always. A mixture of baby powder and the grapes she was surrounded by every day. "Everything is going to be okay," she whispered into my hair. "Do what they say and come home to us. I don't care who you love. Okay? Remember that. My parents cared. Didn't like my...friend...and forced me to marry your dad. I don't want that for you. I love you and only want you to be happy." She lifted my chin and peered into my eyes, which were wet with unshed tears.

I nodded, unable to speak after hearing her whispered confession. She kissed the top of my head.

Daddy waited at the door. He cleared his throat, uncomfortable with any kind of emotion or physical affection. "Take care, Ivy."

With one final reassuring smile from Momma, the door closed behind them.

23

NOW

"Look at me. *Look at me.* Come on, now." JT pounded into Deadgirl's pussy. The gag was back in her mouth. Other than the occasional grunt, she was unresponsive.

Hearing the door open, JT turned and saw Wheeler. Increasing the speed of this thrusts, he said, "Yeah, you fucking like that, don't you, you fucking dead little zombie cunt. Yeah. I know you like it, corpse."

His strokes became shorter. Harder.

"I'm comin'." He groaned loudly. "Ohhhh, yeah!"

Jumping off the bed, he pulled up his pants.

Wheeler grinned. "How's our hole doing, man?"

"Unwilling but able, as always." Pushing aside a bunch of beer cans and cigarette butts, JT sat on the floor and leaned against the wall, still out of breath. "We gotta, uh…we gotta get some lube or something in there." He pulled out a cigarette and lit it. "She is just bone dry, and I'm gettin' dehydrated from spitting."

Wheeler looked serious for a change. "What do you think she is, JT?"

"Our fuck slave?"

"I mean, seriously, like, I don't know, man." He paced. "Like, what is she doing here and how did she get here?"

Frustrated by the questions, JT got in Wheeler's face. "I don't know, Wheeler. Who fucking cares? Look at her!" He motioned to the girl. "She's perfect. Well, except for the bullet holes and stuff. Otherwise, she's the perfect woman, man. Hot. Naked. Unable to talk. And *ours*. So what's your problem?"

"Nothing! I'm just...asking, ya know? She's weird. This whole thing is weird. She doesn't eat. She doesn't piss. She doesn't shit..." JT's glare made him back down. Figuring he should change the topic, he asked, "How long have you been here, anyway?"

"I spent the night. Why?" JT's voice was surprisingly soft.

"Because it's starting to stink," Wheeler said, matter-of-factly.

Sighing, JT said, "C'mon."

Wheeler followed him to Deadgirl. He stood on one side, JT stood on the other.

After giving her nipple a solid pinch, then walking his fingers across her abdomen, JT squeezed one of the bullet holes. Thick, green pus oozed out. Wrinkling his nose, he said, "*That* is coming from the wounds. I smelled it this morning."

"What the *fuck*?" Wheeler asked, covering his nose.

"A little worse for the wear, but, uh..." He sunk his middle finger into the hole, up to his knuckle. "It's warm. Wet."

Wheeler laughed uncertainly. "Yeahhhh?"

"This one's mine, but there's two more just like it," JT responded playfully.

"Okay." This time Wheeler's laugh was genuine...and naughty.

24

THEN

"Hello, Ivy. I'm Dr. Leonard Bagshaw. Please have a seat." He motioned to the chair in front of his desk.

I plopped down, hiding a yawn behind my hand. It was hard to sleep when the woman in the room next door sang showtunes all night, and the girl across the hall masturbated and orgasmed loudly over and over again.

"All settled in?"

I shrugged, studying him. Mid-forties, tall, trim, pointy nose, salt and pepper hair...a wedding band on his finger. "I guess. I didn't bring much." Which was good, given the size of my room...and the lack of a closet.

"Excellent!" He shuffled through some folders on his desk, pulling out the same brown folder the grumpy, old bitch had carried with her yesterday. Opening it, he studied the paperwork. "So, it seems you have homosexual tendencies?" He peered at me over the black rims of his glasses.

"If you're asking if I like girls, the answer is yes." I lifted my chin defiantly. "That doesn't make me sick."

"Well, of course you'd think that. It feels normal to you, right? But, alas, homosexuality is a disease that we have the means to cure. While there are many philosophies and theories as to why people become homosexual, it's my belief that something happened to you during your childhood. Something that traumatized you to the point of blocking your heterosexual pathway." He gave me a kind smile. "My job is to unclutter that path and put you on the road to normality. To a happy life with a husband and children."

I wanted to puke. "Good fuckin' luck with that."

Ignoring me, he went on. "You have three other siblings, one of which is an identical twin. Interesting. All are heterosexual, yes?"

"As far as I know. We don't make it a habit of discussing our sexual practices around the dinner table."

"Of course," he mumbled, reading the paperwork. "Of course."

"Can I go back to my room now?" I was hungry and wanted breakfast, but I had no idea if meals were served in our rooms, or if there was a cafeteria, or what. Mary hadn't been inclined to show me around yesterday.

"Not quite yet. I need some more information from you. Although your family doctor gave me your medical history and approved your admission here, there are things general practitioners don't know to ask in cases like this."

"Dr. Coffman *approved* this?" I gaped. "But I haven't seen him in years!"

"That's not what his notes say." He walked to a tea service tray sitting in the corner of the room. "Would you like some oolong? It's my belief that there's nothing some nice, aromatic tea can't fix."

"Good. I'll drink away the gay and you can discharge me."

Dr. Bagshaw chuckled. "You're a spicy one, aren't you, Ivy?" Handing me a cup, he shuffled back behind his desk. "I'm going to ask you a series of questions, and I'd like you to answer them as honestly as possible. It will help me fine-tune your treatments."

"Fine," I said, taking a sip of the tea, which was surprisingly good. I just wanted to get this over with.

"Okay, let's get started." Dr. Bagshaw picked up a pen. "How old were you when you first realized you were homosexual?"

"I've felt that way since my first memories. Maybe three or four."

"Good." He scribbled some notes. "Did anything traumatic happen to you as a child that you recall?"

"Other than having a physically abusive father, a doormat mother, a bitchy older sister, and an evil troll for a baby brother? No. The best part of my life has always been Lily, my twin, but, you know…we don't choose our families."

"Physically abusive, you say?"

I held up my arm, covered in an ugly cast. "Yep."

"Interesting. I never picked that up during our phone calls."

"His public persona is nothing like his private one," I answered pragmatically.

"And your mother just goes along with whatever he says?"

I hesitated. I loved Momma, and it seemed we once had much in common. But she'd become a mousy, subservient woman who refused to stand up to Daddy, even to protect her children. "Yes."

"Good, Ivy. Thank you for your honesty, so far." He tapped the pen against his lip. "The questions are going to become a little more personal now."

"Just get on with it," I grumbled.

"When was the first time you engaged in homosexual behavior?"

I didn't even have to think. "My best friend, Eva, and I showed each other our private parts when we were five. Does that count?"

"Indeed. Did anything else happen with you and Eva through the years?"

"We eventually touched each other."

Dr. Bagshaw leaned forward in his chair. "Where?"

"You know," I said, slightly uncomfortable by his intense interest. "All the naughty bits."

"Are you referring to breasts, vaginas, and buttocks?"

I blushed. "Yeah."

"And did you kiss each other?" His breathing was becoming heavier.

"All the time, when we knew it was safe."

"Tell me, Ivy, did you orgasm before you were ten?"

"Yes." I didn't elaborate.

"And what brought you to orgasm?"

"Uh, several things." I set the teacup on his desk. "Is this really necessary?"

"The more I know, the quicker we can fix the issue, and the sooner you can go home."

Sighing, I said, "Her…finger playing with me."

"On your clitoris?"

"Yes."

"Above or below the underwear?"

"Below."

"And did she insert her finger inside you?"

"Eventually." I noticed the hand not holding the pen drop behind the desk.

"Did you also bring her to orgasm implementing those same techniques?"

"I did."

The sound of a zipper…*unzipping*…filled the room.

"And did you perform cunnilingus on each other?"

I was mesmerized by his arm moving slowly up and down behind the desk. Was he for real? Very uncomfortable and wanting nothing more than to leave, I blurted, "Yes."

"How old were you?"

"Maybe twelve or thirteen."

His arm moved faster. "Did you like it?"

Near tears, I said, "Yes."

"Giving or receiving?"

"Both, okay? I liked both!" I jumped up and ran from the room, but not before hearing the groan as he climaxed.

25

NOW

Rickie hated gym class. He sat on the bleachers, deep in thought, as the rest of his classmates played basketball. When a ball bounced across the gym and hit his knee, he grabbed it and glanced up…at JoAnn.

She smiled.

He returned the smile but said nothing.

After a moment of confused hesitation, JoAnn said, "What are you looking at?"

He grinned lazily. "You."

Tilting her head, she replied playfully, "No, you're not."

Chuckling, Rickie bounced the ball back to her.

She caught it, started to leave, then paused. "Hey, remember that time when we were like, eight, or something?"

"Eight?"

She giggled. "Okay, eight, nine, whatever. Just let me finish."

"We were twelve," he said.

"What? How do you remember that?" She giggled. "Was I your first kiss, or something?"

He looked down, his smile turning uncomfortable. "Hey, um, you wanna go out with me sometime?"

Surprised by his abruptness, she shrugged noncommittally. "That was a *long* time ago. I mean, another life."

He stared at his shoes.

"Nothing lasts forever, Rickie."

He watched her walk away.

* * *

UR DEAD, FAGET was written in bold, black letters across Rickie's locker. Ignoring the message, he opened the door and reached for his backpack. A hand slapping his shoulder caused him to spin around defensively.

"Fuck, man," he said to Wheeler.

"Whoa! Take it easy, bro!" Wheeler grinned good-naturedly.

Rickie slammed his locker shut. "Sorry. Just a little tense."

"Nice," Wheeler said, tapping his finger against the scrawled message.

"Yeah, funny, huh?"

They went outside, heading across the parking lot to the bike racks.

"I'm going over to the nuthouse. Wanna come?" Wheeler asked.

"I want nothing more to do with that shit. I'm not going back."

"C'mon, man. Why not? It would make JT happy."

"I could not give less of a shit about making JT happy."

"But we're, like, the Three Musketeers, man! 'All for one,' and all that bullshit."

"Nah. We were, man, but JT fucked it up. I'm done."

"Fuck, dude..." Wheeler started to say before a fist came out of nowhere, punching him in the nose.

Rickie watched him fall to the ground an instant before a fist connected with his own face.

"Fuck!" Rickie grabbed his jaw.

"You get the message, shit stain?" Johnny asked, chest-butting Rickie. Dwyer stood nearby, laughing.

"What the fuck, man?"

Johnny kneed him in the gut. "What's that, pussy? You think I can't see you when you're staring and drooling over JoAnn?"

* * *

Sitting on the hood of Dwyer's car, Sophie took a drag from her cigarette and let out a tired sigh. "Oh, God. What are they doing *now?*"

JoAnn turned to look toward the commotion, her smile vanishing when she realized what was happening.

* * *

"Fuck off," Rickie mumbled.

"Shut your filthy mouth, man. Just shut the fuck up!" Spittle flew from Johnny's mouth.

Wheeler scrambled to his feet. "You're an asshole!" Grabbing Rickie's backpack, he swung it at Johnny's head.

Johnny caught the bag in one hand and hit Wheeler with the other, knocking him on his ass. More blood gushed from his broken nose.

"All right, you little shits," Johnny declared. "One last time. *Keep your eyes to yourself!*"

Pushing himself to his knees, Rickie said, "I don't know what the fuck you're talking about."

"Is that right?" Johnny kicked him in the ribs. "Maybe that'll help you remember."

"Fuck!" Rickie cried out, curling his body into the fetal position.

"Johnny, stop!" JoAnn rushed over. "Johnny!"

He ignored her. "No more looking at my woman, you little shit. You got that?"

"Stop!" JoAnn was near tears. "Johnny, knock it off! That's enough, okay? I want to go home."

Instantly contrite, Johnny said, "Come on, baby, I'm just defending your honor over here."

"No, you're not. You're being an asshole." JoAnn said, disgusted.

Johnny looked at the gathered crowd, embarrassed to be chastised by a girl.

Wheeler, not ready to let it go, dove for Dwyer. Seeing the coming attack, he sidestepped, avoiding the hit, but punched Wheeler in the face, sending him sprawling into JoAnn. Unable to catch herself, she fell on top of Rickie. Face-to-face, they locked eyes for a moment before Johnny pulled her up.

"Stop it! Get off me!" She slapped his hands away.

"Look, we're just having a little fun! That's all!"

JoAnn gave him a firm shove. "Just stop." She glanced at Rickie writhing on the ground with regret. "I'm sorry," she mouthed, then walked away.

"Now look what you did, you fucking creep!" Johnny yelled. "You fucking pissed off my girl!" He spat a wad of phlegm onto Rickie's chest.

Laughing, Johnny and Dwyer gave each other a high five, then sauntered off.

Wheeler crawled toward Rickie, his nose dripping crimson droplets along the blacktop. "You okay?" Seeing that Rickie was in agony and unable respond, in a burst of ill-timed, self-righteous anger, he hollered after them, "Fuck you, you fucking jock motherfuckers!"

Johnny and Dwyer stopped in their tracks, turning with amused expressions.

Wheeler wasn't finished. "You fuckers! We don't need your fucking cheerleading whores! You know why? Because we got our own fucking whore, and she's the sweetest one in the whole fucking town, you assholes!"

Johnny and Dwyer exchanged a glance.

"She's got fucking sweet tits, and she's fucking hot!" Wheeler was out-of-control, barely coherent with rage.

Desperate to quiet him, Rickie struggled to sit up. "Wheeler, shut the fuck up!" He grabbed him by the arm, trying to calm him down, but Wheeler wouldn't stop.

"So fuck you, jock boys! She's *our* fucking sex slut!"

The jocks approached again, fists clenched.

26

THEN

"All right, Miss Reyes. We're going to start your aversion therapy today," Clara, the nice dayshift nurse said, drawing clear fluid into a syringe.

My stomach growled. The food here was one step up from pet food. I'd barely eaten for days.

Clara chuckled. "That's one hungry belly. After this, you won't wanna eat the rest of the day, girl. Maybe not tomorrow either."

"Wow, really?" Not knowing what aversion therapy was, I was shocked.

"Yep, really." Clara said. She was short, round like a potato, had dyed black hair with several inches of gray roots, and was old enough to be my grandmother. Within these walls, she was the best friend I had.

"Darn," I said, looking dejected. "I was really looking forward to today's menu of sewer rat marinated in castor oil, with a side of grasshopper pudding."

"Don't be silly. You know those fine Linda Vista chefs are making eel loaf with a side of jellied moose nose."

I giggled. Clara had a sharp wit I appreciated. "So how does this work?" I gestured to the supplies.

"It's pretty simple, really. Dr. Bagshaw selected a group of photographs for you to look at. But before you do, I have to inject you with this here emetic." She held up the syringe. "It's a drug that makes you increasingly nauseous, to the point you'll start vomiting. A lot."

"Oh," I said, suddenly gloomy. "That sounds awful."

"That's the point, darlin'. That's the point."

"Clara?"

"Yes, dear?"

"I don't think I'm sick." My voice was small.

She leaned down and whispered into my ear. "Neither do I. I think you're perfect just as you are."

I gave her a grateful smile.

"You ready?"

"Let's do it." I sighed.

She administered the emetic just below my skin...what she called a 'subcutaneous injection.'

"Now we need to wait five minutes or so. When you start feeling nauseous, let me know."

I was feeling it after two minutes...dizzy, sweaty, flushed. Clara handed me a stack of photos, all of beautiful naked women. Sometimes alone, sometimes doing things with other women. By the fourth photo, I was projectile vomiting. By the seventh, I seriously thought I was going to die. There must have been a hundred photos, and I had to look at each and every one...while feeling like death.

It was the single worst experience of my life.

The next day, Dr. Bagshaw asked me how I felt about women.

"If there was one standing here right now, I'd fuck her," I said, licking my lips.

The look on his face made the gallons of vomit worth it.

27

NOW

Wheeler hiccupped, then sniffled loudly as the engine in Johnny's car roared beneath them. When Dwyer had threatened to knock their teeth out, Wheeler gave up the address, then Johnny had locked them inside the trunk. Now they were on their merry way to the nuthouse, thanks to fucking Wheeler's crazed outburst.

Dude had the audacity to sniffle again. Pissed, Rickie clenched his fists.

"Shut the fuck up, Wheeler! I'll punch you myself if you don't stop the fucking boo-hooing. Johnny's going to take one fucking look at Deadgirl, and he's going to turn around and fucking bust us, man. You understand that?"

Wheeler started crying again. "I'm sorry, Rickie. I'm so sorry," he blubbered.

"Great. You're sorry. That will unfuck us for sure." Rickie felt around the trunk for a weapon, but there was nothing... except a slimy used condom. Wiping his fingers on the carpet, he prayed it wasn't from an evening with JoAnn. "If we don't fucking come up with something right now, we're going to go to fucking jail, Wheeler."

"Rickie, man, I can't go to jail." His voice was whiny, baby-ish. "My fucking mom would kill me!" His cries turned to sobs.

"Stop! Stop! Look, whatever happens, we *cannot show them Deadgirl*, okay? It can't happen! I cannot stress this enough. We keep this between us, and you keep your mouth shut, okay?"

The car slowed, and the brakes squealed to a stop.

"Oh, shit. Shit, shit, shit!" Wheeler muttered.

Two car doors opened and closed. Two sets of footsteps walked around the car and stopped at the trunk. From outside, they heard Johnny's voice. "All right, you little fuckwads. Don't even think about making a run for it. Dwyer's got a baseball bat, and he's a fucking state champ. Got it?"

Wheeler whimpered. And sniffled.

* * *

They walked down the long, dark hallway, Rickie and Wheeler in front, Johnny and Dwyer—who had his trusty baseball bat resting against his shoulder—bringing up the rear.

"C'mon, you guys. Wheeler was just fucking talking shit. I swear to God, there's *nothing* down here." Rickie was desperate.

"Talking shit, huh?" Johnny gave Rickie a shove. "I guess Dwyer and I can stop fucking around and kick your asses right now then, huh? Huh?"

Rickie glanced back. Johnny and Dwyer, both wearing mani-acal grins, were twitching with energy and unspent rage, itching to get violent. Knowing it would likely end badly for him, he still decided to use that rage to distract them from Deadgirl.

Stopping dead in his tracks, he turned and raised his fists, ready to fight. "Yeah. I guess you're gonna have to."

After a moment of tension, Johnny grinned delightedly at Dwyer, who laughed at Rickie.

"You really are an idiot, aren't you?" Dwyer palmed the bat. "Only bringing fists to a bat fight."

Determined, Rickie remained in the boxer's stance.

"Fuck you!" Dwyer screamed, plunging the blunt end of the bat hard into Rickie's gut.

Rickie fell to the ground, blacking out from the pain.

28

THEN

Dear Diary,

My days pass in a blur of hunger, sleep deprivation, and pain from skin infections. They only allow us to shower once a week, and our linens are never washed. Mine are crusty with menstrual blood (pads are hard to come by around here, so I'm often forced to stuff toilet paper into my panties and hope for the best) and vomit from the endless aversion therapies I've been subjected to. I thought about removing the sheets and sleeping only on the mattress, but I'd rather sleep in my own bodily fluids than those of the people who came before me.

I've lost weight. My clothes hang on my frame. At least I'm able to wash them myself in the bathroom sink, using the pubic hair-covered bars of soap we all share. It's gross, but it's my only option. I drape them over the few pieces of furniture in my room until they dry. I never can get all the soap out, so they always feel stiff and itchy, but it's better than wearing something filthy.

My birthday came and went without a peep from my family. No recognition from the staff either. Well, except for Clara. She brought me a few leftover cookies she'd made at home for her grandkids. They were chocolate no-bake cookies, and they were the most delicious things I've ever eaten. A New Year's Eve baby, I saved them until the clock struck midnight, and 1945 rolled into 1946. A combination birthday/New Year's celebration.

The woman in the room next to me has switched from showtunes to country ballads. I'm not sure which is worse. There is one bit of good news…the orgasm-girl from across the hall was moved to another floor. The elderly lady in there now sleeps around the clock, so things are somewhat quieter.

They cut off my cast a while back. My arm is withered and pale, the muscle tone non-existent. I don't take in enough calories to build it back up again, so I guess I'll stay lopsided until I ditch this joint.

Dr. Bagshaw is a walking erection. I can't turn my head without making him hard. It is repulsive and scary and completely inappropriate. I've stopped answering his questions honestly during our interviews. Instead, I make up random gibberish like, "The snake wore mittens in the summer snow." He still writes it down, as if it's the secret to unlocking my psyche, while masturbating the entire time. He keeps trying the emetic sessions, but the only thing it has ever managed to do is get me out of cafeteria duty. We all take turns serving the food and washing the dishes. It isn't much fun, but it's better than sitting inside my locked room for hours on end. I have no friends here.

I miss Lily.

I miss Carrie.

I miss my freedom.

I miss…living.

29

NOW

Rickie regained consciousness sprawled across the floor of the sub-basement. He was alone. The pain in his gut was unbearable, but he had to find Wheeler before he took Johnny and Dwyer to Deadgirl. Slowly crawling to his feet, he lumbered down the hallway, cradling his abdomen.

Wheeler stood outside Deadgirl's opened door, shoulders hunched, eyes fixed on the ground. "I'm sorry," he said, his voice flat and resigned.

Defeated, Rickie slid down the wall and didn't move.

* * *

Johnny and Dwyer ogled Deadgirl's unmoving body in stunned silence. They slowly approached, their eyes exploring every inch of her exposed flesh.

"Jesus," Dwyer finally whispered.

Johnny looked at Deadgirl, then back at Dwyer, then back at Deadgirl before uttering, "What…the…*fuck*?"

"See?" came Wheeler's nasally voice from behind them. "She's right there, just like I said." He pushed a bloody rag against his broken nose.

Dwyer turned to Wheeler, his tone flat. "What the fuck is this?"

"It's just what it looks like, Dwyer," said JT, lounging in a ratty recliner, one leg crossed over the other, in a dark corner of the room. He wore nothing but a black zip-up hoodie, red underwear, and a pair of well-worn black boots. A long, silver necklace hung around his neck. The small table beside him held empty beer cans, bags of chips and popcorn, and a deck of cards. A faded orange sleeping bag lay wadded at his feet. "Hot-to-trot bitch with a yen for dick."

"JT," Johnny said, startled by his unexpected appearance.

JT took a long drag of his cigarette. "Johnny," he replied stoically. The scratches on his face were raw, bloody…a stark contrast to his pale complexion. Dark purple-hued circles rimmed his eyes. "So, you boys decided to come by and give our girlfriend a ride, huh?"

"Uh, no. We were just fucking around with Wheeler, all right?" For the first time, Johnny seemed off his game, recognizing it was now three against two. "I thought he was shitting us."

"Ain't no shittin' going on here, boy." JT was confident, in control.

"What *is* going on here, JT?" Dwyer asked timidly, studying Deadgirl. "Why's she all tied up and beat to shit?"

"Because that's the way she *likes it*, Dwyer." JT stood up, resting the bolt cutters Rickie had left behind on his shoulder, an obvious mockery of the other boy. "Rough! S&M!"

Johnny backed away, nervous.

"Ain't either of you seen any pornos before?" JT continued, banging the bolt cutters against a pipe. "That's the way we give it to her. You know, whips and chains and shit?" Rubbing his hand along Deadgirl's breast, he repeated, "Yeah, that's the way we give it to her."

She shifted, responding to his touch.

"See? She's hot for it."

Johnny looked terrified.

"You all want to, uh…" JT motioned to Deadgirl and winked.

"Nah, man. We're…we're fine, thanks." Johnny stammered, then looked at Dwyer. "We're fine, Dwyer. Ain't going in there." He paused, his expression fearful. "We should leave."

JT smirked, amused. "Two red-blooded, all-American studs like you passing on free pussy? Guess what they say about tight ends is true."

"Fuck you," Dwyer said. He walked around the table inspecting Deadgirl's body. "I don't know."

Rickie entered the room, his face covered in bruises, silently taking everything in.

"Look, I know you boys have a little problem with my compadre here," JT said, throwing his arm over Wheeler's shoulders. "But I'm willing to let bygones be bygones. Know what I mean?"

"Nah, man," Wheeler whined. "Let them find their own snatch! She's ours!"

JT glared at Wheeler, warning him to shut up. "C'mon, fellas! The more the merrier!" He pinched Deadgirl's nipple, causing her to moan.

"Just shut the fuck up *for once*, okay, Wheeler?" Rickie whispered.

Dwyer ran his finger along Deadgirl's calf and shrugged. "I mean, what the fuck?" He handed Johnny the bat.

"Dwyer, no."

"Come on, Johnny."

"What are you doing?"

"Don't leave me hanging here, man." Dwyer unzipped his fly, stepped between her legs, and pushed himself inside. He grunted as their flesh slapped together. "Oh, yeah. C'mon in, Johnny. The water's fine!"

JT grinned.

"What?" Johnny asked angrily. "And dip my wick in a

puddle of your spunk? I may be horny, but I'm not desperate. After all," he turned and looked directly at Rickie, a self-satisfied smirk on his face. "I got my own sweet pussy waiting for me tonight."

Glaring, Rickie said, "Yeah? Why don't you go for the mouth then?"

30

THEN

I screamed just before the electrical shock ripped through my body.

When I came to, my head was pounding. "Where am I?" I screeched, afraid. "And who are you?" I asked the woman standing beside me.

Later, I realized it was Clara, but at that moment, my brain felt like scrambled eggs. Nothing made sense, and I couldn't remember anything. Instead of the shifting images I normally envisioned with memory recall, I saw only gray. Nauseous, I vomited a stream of yellow bile onto the floor and immediately fell asleep.

Dr. Bagshaw had decided it was time to advance to the next step in my treatments: electroconvulsive therapy. "I'm going to send a precisely placed electrical impulse into your brain," he'd told me a week ago. "It will stimulate a controlled seizure. When you wake up, if all goes as planned, you'll be cured!"

"Sounds like bullshit," I'd said with more bravado than I felt. "And 'if all goes as planned?' What the hell is that? No faith in your skills as a physician, huh?" I snorted. "Join the club."

He liked it when I was angry. It turned him on. But it was only when he stood and dropped his pants around his ankles, his tiny erection rigid and perpendicular to his body, that I ran from his office.

"Girl, you shoulda been put under general anesthesia for that procedure," Clara told me later. "But that evil man doesn't think it's necessary. Can you believe that? It's painful! I know you don't remember it, but you screamed and screamed." Her face crumpled and tears ran down her cheeks as she paced agitatedly around my room. "And you had a massive seizure that lasted far longer than it should. I begged Bagshaw to give you some medicine to make it stop, but he wouldn't. You could have died!"

I was horrified by the information, but what could I do? I was a prisoner within these crumbling walls, my body a play-thing for immoral and corrupt doctors and nurses.

"I need to quit this stinkin' job," Clara mumbled. But I knew she couldn't. She supported her daughter and three of her grandchildren on a very meager salary.

"Do my parents know what he is doing to me, Clara?"

"No idea, sugar. No idea."

"As awful as Daddy is, I can't imagine he'd let them risk my life. Especially for such ineffective treatments!"

I know I could have lied. Praised Bagshaw's genius. Told him I wanted nothing more than to go home and find myself a good, strong man to care for me and give me ten children. But even if I did, he wouldn't discharge me. I knew that as clearly as I knew my hair was brown. I was his plaything. His fantasy girl. He had no intention of giving me up.

There was also a baser reason for my continued honesty. I liked pointing out how ineffective his ridiculous treatments were. What a lousy doctor he was. How little he knew about homosexuality.

Because, at the end of the day…I still liked girls.

"Well," Dr. Bagshaw said, when he found out, "I guess we need to do another round."

"What if I refuse?"

"You don't have that authority, Ivy. As a committed patient, it's my responsibility to decide what's best for you. Your preferences are of little importance."

"That's bullshit! I'm of sound mind!" I stood, slapping my hands against the surface of his desk. "There isn't a damn thing wrong with me!"

"You're a female who sexually craves other females." He puffed a cigar that looked and smelled like a turd. "You are most certainly not of sound mind."

Furious, I walked the endless hallways. As I passed a treatment room, I saw a little girl, no more than twelve years old, looking at the same naughty images I'd been shown, and vomiting into a metal basin. *This place is going to destroy us all.*

31

NOW

"She likes it any way she can get it, Johnny-boy." Rickie said.

Hearing Rickie's voice, Deadgirl fixed her gaze on him.

"What's the matter, man?" Rickie goaded. "You scared? Or is she just out of your league?"

JT's eyes widened in surprise, but he stayed silent.

Cornered, Johnny looked around the room, gauging reactions. Aside from Dwyer, who was too busy with the girl to pay attention, the others looked smug.

"I bet JoAnn doesn't do that for you." Rickie was on a roll. "You know what, Johnny? I bet you're full of shit. I bet you haven't had your dick sucked your whole life. I bet you never—"

"Hey!" Johnny interrupted. "Can't deny the lady, now, can we?" He threw the bat at Wheeler, who was barely able to catch it before it dropped to the floor.

"You the man, Johnny!" Dwyer yelled, fucking Deadgirl harder. "You the man!"

Johnny moved apprehensively to the head of the gurney. Deadgirl's eyes rolled back, and she moaned. Looking nervously at Rickie, Johnny unbuttoned his pants. They fell to his ankles. Moving in closer, he said, "Come on, baby. It's all right. It's not gonna bite you."

JT choked back a laugh.

Thrusting his hips forward, he fucked the girl's mouth, relaxing immediately as he realized how good it felt. She gagged continuously, straining against her bonds.

"Whoa! She's a hellcat!" Johnny said, getting into it. "Ain't you a hellcat, sweetie?"

Dwyer whooped as his cock slammed hard into her pussy. "Damn, Johnny! We're spit-roasting her! She's a sweet one!"

"She's got some sweet, sweet lips on her, that's for sure," Johnny said, going deep-throat. "Ahh, yeah! She's like a fucking Dyson!"

Sickened and ashamed, Rickie grabbed Johnny's shoulder. "Okay, man. That's enough!"

Johnny shoved him away. "Yeah? Get in line, fag."

"Stop that," Rickie said, trying again to pull him from her.

Johnny stopped thrusting, a glazed look in his eyes. Brows furrowed, he cried out, and not in the good way. "Oh! Ahhhhhhhhhh! Jesus Christ, she's biting me! *She's biting me!*"

The girl growled.

"Oh, shit! Oh shit!" Dwyer said, pulling out.

"Bitch! Bitch! Bitch! Fucking bitch!" Johnny shrieked, pummeling the girl's face. When she finally released him, he fell to the ground, sobbing, blood spurting from his mangled penis.

Dwyer helped him up. "I'm taking him to the hospital, then we're calling the cops!"

JT jumped in. "And tell them *what*? That he was raping a chick in the mouth, and she bit his dick?"

Crying and groping himself, Johnny blubbered, "I wasn't raping her! You said she wanted it!"

Deadgirl snapped her teeth.

JT sneered. "Yeah, well. I'm sure they heard that one before."

"You said she liked it," Dwyer argued, still trying to assist Johnny.

"Get off me, man," Johnny wailed, cradling his mutilated manhood.

"Prove it in court when Johnny-boy here whips his dick out." JT looked at the girl's broken and bloodied face. "Prove it when they show photos of her."

Rickie was ready to throw up.

JT continued his badgering. "And hey, don't forget about JoAnn, huh? How are you going to explain this to her? 'Well, gee, honey. I was just walking through this abandoned mental hospital, and my weenie was hanging out, and I tripped and fell, and guess where it ended up?'"

"That's bullshit," Johnny protested, still kneeling on the floor. "Look what she did to me!"

"Look at him, man! He's fucking bleeding!" Dwyer added, panicked.

"It ain't as bad as it seems. You were hard, man. All that blood was rushing down there." JT's voice was mocking. "I tell you what though, you hold off on sticking it to JoAnn for a couple weeks, you'll be right as rain. You tell her you're saving your strength for the state championships, or whatever the fuck it is you do."

"Fuck you, man," Johnny said, still sobbing.

"Go to the cops," JT said. "Send me and Rickie and Wheeler to jail...and yourselves." He smiled. "You won't be fit to tackle a dim-witted little girl with polio by the time you get out." Suddenly serious, his voice quieted. "Me and the boys? Well, we'll miss a couple of divorces, a handful of brats, and about a million shifts at the gas station."

Rickie felt as though he'd been punched in the gut. Wheeler looked bummed by JT's assessment.

"See, jail is full of motherfuckers like us," JT continued. "We got nothing to lose...not like the two of you."

"Don't touch me," Johnny whined to Dwyer. "Get off me! Get off me!"

"You're not going to get away with this, JT!" Dwyer

shouted.

"You're not gonna get away with this, JT," he mimicked. "You fuckin' stupid prick. Get the fuck outta here. Go on! Do whatever you want, just get the fuck outta here. Johnny's dripping nasty jock blood all over my nice basement."

"Fuck you, man!" Dwyer responded, grabbing his bat from Wheeler as he dragged a whimpering Johnny from the room. "Fuck you!"

32

THEN

"Clara, something's wrong. My chest doesn't feel right." I leaned against the wall to keep from falling.

"Okay," she said calmly. "Let me grab a wheelchair, and we'll take you to the sick bay." She helped me slide down the wall to the floor. "Do not move. I'll be back in a jif."

"Okay," I said, my voice tiny. I couldn't seem to take a deep breath, and I was very light-headed.

Ten minutes later, a physician had electrodes on my chest and was monitoring my heart. "Looks like you're in supraventricular tachycardia, Ivy." He wasn't wearing a name tag, but he seemed kind.

"And?" I had no idea what that was.

"It can sometimes happen, but usually isn't a big deal long-term. I'm going to give you some medicine to slow down your heart rate, and we'll keep an eye on it for the next few weeks. Has anything unusual happened recently?"

"Electroconvulsive therapy two days ago. Her second round," Clara said. "She's Bagshaw's patient."

"Ah. Well, that explains a lot. Seizures can cause the electrical activity inside your heart to go a little haywire. Here," he said, handing me a tiny white pill and a glass of cold water.

"Take this, we'll monitor you for a few hours, and if it works as I expect it will, you'll be free to go."

"Thanks, Will," Clara said, exhaling a long sigh. "I was worried."

Will. His name was Will. I tried to keep track of the good ones.

"Not a problem. That's what I'm here for."

"Yes, thank you," I said, greedily sipping the icy water. "It's nice to talk to a doctor who doesn't play with himself in front of me." I felt the blood drain from my face as I realized what I'd said. "Shit," I whispered.

Clara gasped, covering her mouth with her hand.

Will looked perturbed. "So that's true, then?"

"Yeah," I said, not making eye contact and wishing like hell I hadn't mentioned it.

"Oh my God, child. I had no idea!" Clara said, gently rubbing my back with the palm of her hand.

"I'd heard rumors, but many of the patients here aren't exactly reliable." Pulling a clean, warm blanket from a metal shelf, Will handed it to me. "Why don't you lie down, Ivy? Try to rest. I'll see what can be done about this."

I wasn't sure if it was the medicine, the lack of oxygen, or what, but I could barely keep my eyes open. "I will. Thank you." The blanket even smelled nice. I wrapped it around me, luxuriating in its softness. As he and Clara headed to another room, I said, "Will?"

"Yes?"

"Please don't tell anyone who told you."

He drew an 'x' over his heart with his finger. "Cross my heart."

I closed my eyes.

33

NOW

"I...I...I'm so sorry." Wheeler rushed toward JT, his face covered in dried blood. "I didn't mean to say anything. It just came out and—"

"A-a-a-a-and stow it, Wheeler." JT said, making fun of his stutter. "You dumb fuck! You two are lucky I was here. Now, at least, they'll keep their mouths shut. They saw my point."

"You *two*?" Rickie protested. "I didn't have anything to do with this shit, man!"

"Your infatuation with JoAnn fuckin' Skinner is the reason why Johnny came down here. *You* are the reason he got bit. And fuck! It's bad enough those two motherfuckers came down here but look at that shit." JT pointed at Deadgirl. She grinned hideously, her lip split open and bleeding. An eye was purple and swollen shut. A broken nose skewed crazily to the right. "Look at her! I'm going to have to put a fucking bag over her head just to get it up."

Rickie shook his head. "We fucked it up, man."

"You know what, Rickie? You know what?" JT's voice got increasingly louder. "Now nobody gets what they want! JoAnn Skinner, man? What the fuck were you thinking? *This* is the best we're ever going to have!"

"What about Johnny and Dwyer?" Wheeler asked.

"They'll stay fucking quiet."

"But what if they don't, JT? I can't fucking go to jail," Wheeler said, whimpering.

"*You're not going to jail!* You're going to get the fuck out of here! You're going to go home, and you're going to go to bed. You're going to wake up tomorrow. You're going to go to school, and you're going to pretend like none of this shit ever happened! So get the fuck out, right now! *Go!*"

Wheeler left, sniffling as he went.

"And you know what?" JT continued, looking at Rickie. "You get the fuck out, too!"

"You're not the fucking boss of this shit!" Rickie got in his face.

JT only looked amused by his outburst. "You are disinvited from my fucking basement, Rick. *You fucked up!*"

Pissed, Rickie stormed out of the room.

Alone, JT closed the door and walked to the bed. The girl stared at the ceiling, smiling serenely. JT grimaced at her train-wreck of a face but stroked her hair.

"Good job, baby. Too bad about the face. At least your other end is still fine."

34

THEN

A year to the day after I was dropped off at the Linda Vista Lunatic Asylum, I found an envelope in my mailroom cubby. There was no return address. Excited, hoping it was from Lily, I rushed upstairs to the third floor, raced inside my room, and slammed the door shut. I wanted to read my very first letter in the privacy of my own space.

Jumping on my bed, which was now covered with the soft blanket Will gave me, I tore open the envelope.

To: Ivy Elizabeth Reyes, Evansburgh, CA
From: Beckford & Clarke, Attorneys at Law
Date: November 8, 1946

Dear Ms. Reyes,

We regret to inform you that your parents, Edgar Philip Reyes and Rosemary Elaine Reyes, in addition to your younger brother, Robert Philip Reyes, were killed in an automobile accident on October 27, 1946. After a memorial service at the Covenant Christian Church on Oakwood Drive, their remains were interred on November 2, 1946, in Tulocay Cemetery in Napa Valley, California. Their will was read the following day on November 3, 1946, at their home. The entirety of your parents' estate was left to one Violet Elaine Reyes.

The only addendum was added by your father in the fall of 1945. He requested you remain at Linda Vista Lunatic Asylum until the time you've been deemed cured by your physicians. The costs associated with your treatments will be covered by the estate.

We, at Beckford & Clarke, are truly sorry for your loss.

Sincerely,

Anthony P. Beckford, Esq.

By the time I reached the end, my eyes were so blurred with tears, I could barely see. Throwing the letter on the floor, I did something patients were forbidden to do. I pushed through the emergency doors leading to the rooftop and breathed fresh air for the first time in twelve months. An alarm sounded, but I didn't care. I needed to breathe, and this was the only way. Running to the ledge, I looked down. Seeing grass and trees and a road leading away from this godforsaken pit helped me feel less confined.

Thank God it wasn't Lily. Thank God it wasn't Lily. Thank God it wasn't Lily. It was as if my brain was stuck on a loop.

But then something else struck me. Where *was* Lily? She was the only family member not mentioned in the letter. Would she stay with Violet? I couldn't imagine that. They'd never gotten along and had very little in common.

Poor Robert. As awful as he often was, he didn't deserve to die before he had a chance to fully live. And Momma, who'd given her life to her husband and family, but who occasionally let me see a flash of the woman she'd once been...a woman very much like me.

For the first time in years, I contemplated prayer. I didn't believe, but I needed something, *anything* to hold on to.

The guards ran onto the roof, halting when they saw me leaning over the railing. "Uh, ma'am, step away from the edge," one of them said.

"Ivy?" I heard Clara's voice and ran into her arms.

"MommaandDaddyandRobert..." It sounded like one run-on word through my sobs.

"I know. I saw the letter in your room. I'm so sorry, baby-girl." She wrapped me in her arms, squeezing tight.

I rested against her, letting the flood of tears come. Eventually, she walked me back into the building and tucked me into bed.

Almost asleep, I was jerked awake by a sudden terrifying thought. Without Daddy to hold the doctors accountable, I was as vulnerable as a baby lamb in the woods. My loud wail echoed throughout the room.

My neighbor banged on the wall. "Shut the fuck up! I'm trying to sing!"

That night, I was submerged in an ice bath for an hour as punishment for breaking the rules.

35

NOW

"JoAnn?" Rickie caught her on her way home from cheerleading practice.

"Rickie?" Her surprise was evident. "What are you doing here?"

"Listen, there's this really, really fucked up situation with Johnny."

"He's an asshole. Okay? I know…I know." She started past him. "After tonight, he'll leave you alone."

"No, he won't."

"Look, I know how you feel about…me, but he's my boyfriend, Rickie" she said. "You're just going to have to deal."

"JoAnn," he sighed. "He doesn't fucking love you."

Unsurprised, she looked away, contemplating his words.

"Listen. Listen, I just…whatever you hear after tonight? I want you to know I tried to fucking stop it, okay? You have to believe me."

"This is…weird, I…" She giggled, glancing nervously around.

"Will you just listen to me? Please?"

"No. What if someone sees us or—"

"What if someone does see us, huh? *What if someone sees us? Who fucking cares?*"

Torn and unable to deal, JoAnn shook her head and walked away.

* * *

JT ate a tuna salad and lettuce sandwich, gazing adoringly at Deadgirl's dangling feet and curled toes. It was sure as hell better than looking at her shattered face.

* * *

Cartoons played on the television set as Clint scooped a huge portion of green bean casserole onto his plate. Leaning back against the couch, he glanced at Rickie sitting beside him. "I hope she's hot."

Rickie looked at him, confused.

"Whoever it is you boys are fightin' over. You're taking a real beating for her. Jesus Christ, man."

Sighing, Rickie spooned some casserole onto his own plate.

"Hey!" Clint said with his mouth full. "Save some for your mom. She'll be home any minute."

Rickie looked at Clint's plate, piled high with more than half the casserole, but remained silent and pushed his plate away.

"You gotta try and relax, man. You've got the rest of your life to carry the weight of the world on your shoulders," Clint continued, talking with his mouth full of food. "You take things way too seriously, son. Be a kid. You know? Have fun." Still chewing, he said, "I tell ya, I really wish I was fifteen again." He chuckled.

"I'm seventeen."

Lost in thought, Clint ignored him. "Man, do I wish I was fifteen again."

On the television, a friendly ghost brought a bird back to life.

* * *

Later that night, mind racing, Rickie tossed and turned on the couch, as JT, flat on his back and hand behind his head, sprawled across his sleeping bag on the basement floor. He stared at the ceiling, smoking cigarette after cigarette.

36

THEN

"Good evening, Ivy." Dr. Bagshaw walked into my room, reeking of alcohol. His tie was draped around his neck, his shirt partially unbuttoned.

"Why are you in my room?" I asked, apprehensive. "I'd like you to leave. Now, please."

"Well, Ivy, we don't always get what we want, do we?" He shut the door behind him, using his master key to lock it. "I certainly didn't want to be fired for inappropriate sexual behavior, but alas, one of my patients made obviously false claims against me, and now I must figure out what to tell my wife. She's going to start in about how I can't support her and the children."

Oh my God. He has children?

"I have no idea what you're talking about." I eased myself from the confines of the bed, moving as far away from him as I could get.

"Funny. Because the hospital board told me that Dr. Will Parvin filed a report alleging I'd exposed myself and masturbated in front of one of my patients." He tapped his chin. "Hm. Who could that be?"

"Any number of them, I'm guessing." I wasn't playing his game.

"Ha! Aren't you clever?" He chuckled. "But I was able to narrow it down, you see. Dr. Parvin filed the paperwork on November 11th...only one day after he saw my star patient in the sick bay." Dr. Bagshaw shuffled drunkenly toward me and booped my nose. "You."

Heart racing, I grabbed the small lamp from my bedside table, and held it aloft. "Get the fuck out of my room before I bash your fucking head in."

"Such language!" He laughed. "Quit being so dramatic, Ivy. I'm just here to administer your final treatment before I go." He ran his finger from my temple to my jaw. I smacked his hand away. "You're a very treatment-resistant patient. Nothing I've tried has worked...*yet*." His eyes were red-rimmed, his breath smelled, and his skin was covered in a sheen of grease. "But you're in luck! I have an ace up my sleeve, you see. The best treatment of all." He unzipped his pants and pushed them down. "We're going to have ourselves a little exposure therapy session." He stroked his erection. "You can touch it. You can smell it. You can lick it, even. You're going to feel it moving inside you, and you're gonna love tasting that sweet, sweet jizz." He snatched the lamp away from me and threw it to the ground. It shattered into hundreds of useless pieces. "And at the end of the night, you're gonna fucking realize just how much you love dick!"

Pushing me face-first onto the bed, he ripped off my panties, and plunged inside me. I screamed so loudly as he pushed through my hymen, my throat constricted. But nobody helped me. As he violated my body, the only sounds were his drunken grunting, and my neighbor singing "Divorce Me C.O.D."

It was Christmas night.

37

NOW

Rickie watched as JoAnn assisted a pale, sickly Johnny down the staircase at school the next morning. Johnny groped his belly as they passed but said nothing.

"Do you think they told anybody?" Wheeler said, stopping on the landing.

"I don't know, man. I think we'd be in a heap of shit right now if they did." Sighing, he looked at Wheeler. "Look, just stay cool, all right? They're not doing anything, man."

Forcing a grin, Wheeler said, "I'm cool, okay? Thank God for JT, you know?"

"JT?" Rickie was incredulous. "You fucking kidding me? If it weren't for fucking JT, none of this shit would have happened in the first place."

"Hey! That's no way to be talking about friends, man."

"I should have fucking torched the whole building the night we found her."

"She's just a Deadgirl, man. That's all." Wheeler said stoically.

"You know what, Wheeler?" Rickie started back up the stairs. "Just leave me the fuck alone."

"Rickie. Rickie! Hey! We gotta stick together!"

Rickie didn't acknowledge him. Realizing he'd yelled a little too loudly, Wheeler glanced apprehensively around, then headed to his next class.

* * *

A bloody bucket of soapy water sat beside the bed as JT washed Deadgirl's face. He gently scrubbed off the dried blood with a damp cloth, then tossed it back into the pail. Blotting her dry with a hand towel, he grabbed the plastic bag he'd hung on the corner of her headboard. Inside was a bright pink blush, a palette of eighties-inspired eye shadows, and a tube of dark red lipstick. It was all he could find in his grandma's medicine cabinet.

"Hold still, baby. I'm trying to fix you up."

He ineptly applied blue eyeshadow, covering her entire lid, then colored round circles on the balls of her cheeks with the garish fuchsia blusher. When he attempted the lipstick, he got more outside the lips than on them.

Standing back to admire his handiwork, he winced. "Motherfucker. You look like a goddamn clown."

Deadgirl's eyes rolled back inside their sockets.

* * *

"Dairy products must be sold by a certain date in order to avoid spoilage, which can lead to serious illness." Ms. Flynn, the home economics teacher, flipped through her photos of cottage cheese, yogurt, and a carton of milk.

Hearing a gurgling sound, followed by a rancid stench, Rickie grimaced and looked around the classroom, trying to figure out what it was and where it was coming from. One row over and several seats back, Johnny had his hands wrapped protectively over his stomach, his skin pasty and sweaty.

"Then, of course, meat." Ms. Flynn continued. The current

slide showed a ribeye steak. "Rotten meat, in particular, when left unrefrigerated, can be toxic. But I'm sure everybody here is very familiar with the safety issues concerning poorly kept perishables."

Johnny's gut rumbled loudly enough for the entire class to hear. JoAnn, sitting in front of him, covered her nose as the smell permeated.

"Johnny, think fast!" Matt, his teammate said, tossing him a football.

It bounced off his stomach, nearly causing him to puke, and dropped uselessly to the floor. Ms. Flynn stopped her presentation, giving the class a warning look, then went on.

"Some examples of perishables are—"

"What's that smell?" Sophie asked, loudly interrupting. She fanned her hand around.

Rickie's face puckered in disgust. It smelled like a dead animal on the side of the road, rotting in the mid-day sun.

Stomach rolling, Johnny rocked back and forth, looking ready to burst into tears. Groaning loudly, he raced from the room, crop-dusting his classmates with his stench. JoAnn looked both concerned and embarrassed.

The men's bathroom door flew open with a bang as Johnny stumbled inside. Running to an empty stall, he unbuttoned his pants, and plopped down on the toilet seat just in time. Beads of perspiration dripped from his face.

"Oh my God..." he muttered, his belly growling even louder. He whimpered in pain and gripped his stomach. "What the fuck?"

Feeling something unusual, he lifted his shirt. His abdomen was covered with a large, swollen, purple football-shaped hematoma. Overcome by his endlessly churning stomach, he dropped his shirt and gripped the rails on either side of the toilet. His groans turned to a coughing fit as he continued to empty his bowels into the toilet bowl.

When it stopped, he sat with his head in his hands.

"What the…?" He sniffed, smelling something coppery and metallic…something more than just shit.

Standing, he reached back and touched his splattered buttocks, covering his fingers with dark, viscous blood. As he stood there, gaping, his guts hemorrhaged explosively, causing blood and tissue to spray all over the wall and toilet. Screaming loud enough for his classmates to hear, he fell to the floor and crawled from the stall on his belly, streaking blood, and dragging his wet, glistening intestines behind him.

38

THEN

Dear Diary,
I want to die.

39

NOW

"Nice of you to visit," JT said, shining his flashlight on Dwyer, whose knife cut the rope keeping Deadgirl tied to the gurney. She was bent over the side, ass ripe for the taking. A magazine photo of a blonde model was taped to her face to hide the unfixable damage. "Though I was expecting someone else..."

"Stand back, JT. I'm taking her with me."

"I don't think so."

Dwyer pointed the knife at him, shading his eyes from the bright light. "Fuck you, man. Johnny's...I don't know what this chick's got, but she's fucking coming with me to the hospital, and we're going to the cops, man."

Unperturbed, JT said. "I've been fucking her for days. So has Wheeler." He paused. "So did you." He shook his head. "There ain't nothing wrong with her."

"Bullshit!" He moved closer, still pointing the knife at JT. "Johnny got his guts stuffed back into him. He doesn't eat. He doesn't sleep. The doctors can't figure out what the fuck is wrong with him. And he's starting to smell like fucking rotten meat, okay?" He grimaced. "He's starting to...he's starting to smell like *her*."

JT's expression changed as a piece of the puzzle fell into place. "She *bit* him," he said with wonder.

"No shit, she bit him. Now stand the fuck back! I'm taking her with me."

"Aw. You don't need to do that," JT said, softly. "See, Johnny's dead."

Tears glistened in Dwyer's eyes. "Fuck you, man. Johnny is *not* dead. He's just really fucking sick."

"Nah. Johnny's dead, dude," JT said, pleased that Johnny was finally receiving his comeuppance.

Disturbed by the inappropriate glee on JT's face, Dwyer took a step back.

Deadgirl, one hand free, lunged and grabbed him. Pulling him toward her, she bit deeply into his ribcage, tearing through the crinkled-up magazine page taped to her face. He screamed and dropped his knife, struggling to free himself. A large chunk of his skin remained wedged between her teeth, as he fell to the ground.

"Guess your head is too used to being inside a helmet, tough guy. Them football pads made you softer than you think you are, Dwyer." JT shined the flashlight on his grisly wound, then picked up the dropped knife. "You just don't get it, do ya? *Johnny* is dead. The *bitch* is dead. Now…*you're* dead, too."

"You're fucking nuts, man! You're fucking nuts!"

"Well…" JT complacently nodded in agreement, then plunged the blade hilt deep into Deadgirl's skull. He lifted her head with the knife's handle, removing the wrinkled magazine photo taped to her face. It was a mess of bruises and severe swelling, her features horribly disfigured. Dark blood dribbled down her chin. "You'll like being dead. Deadgirl likes it, don't you?"

Eyes closed, she moaned.

Shocked by the violence, Dwyer tried to scream, but only produced a faint whimper. Weakening, he inched his way to the door.

Grabbing Dwyer by his ankles, JT pulled him back. "Didn't know what I was going to do after you boys messed her up. But now I know. One bite from her and I can make another!"

Dwyer grabbed one of the many pipes that extended from floor to ceiling with both hands, trying to stop JT's momentum.

"Let it go, Dwyer! Get off there!" JT kicked him once. Then again. "Just get off there! Why ya being such a fucking pansy, jock-boy? I expected more."

Losing his grip, Dwyer screamed piteously as JT slid him the rest of the way across the floor and presented him to Deadgirl. "Still hungry, baby?"

40

THEN

On New Year's Day, 1947, a new doctor, Wolfgang Gerhard, arrived at Linda Vista. He was a short, lean man, maybe an inch or so taller than my five-foot, seven-inch frame. Dark hair was combed straight back, as though flaunting his receding hairline. Warm brown eyes, heavy brow bones, and a goofy, gap-toothed grin had me hoping for better days ahead.

"You have an accent!" I said during our first meeting. I was thrilled. Maybe homosexuality wasn't looked as poorly upon in other countries. Maybe he'd send me home.

"Yes," he said with a charming smile. "I'm originally from Bavaria but have lived in the United States for ten years."

"Do you still have family there?"

"Yes. I do." He looked uncomfortable.

"I hope they're safe. I've gotta say, I'm so glad the war is over. I cry every time I think about the concentration camps. What was done to those poor people..."

"Indeed." He cleared his throat. "So tell me about yourself, Ivy."

Trying to win him over, I said, "I'm a Capricorn. I love good wine, especially Pinot, and my type is tanned and blonde...with a nice pair!" When he didn't laugh, I added my usual line...the thing about me that always fascinated folks the most. "I'm an identical twin."

It worked on Dr. Gerhard, too. He leaned forward in his chair, "Oh, really? Fascinating. I've been studying twins most of my adult life."

"Most people can't tell us apart. We're identical in every way. But once you get to know us, it's very clear who is who. Lily is quiet, shy, loves to read, and is slow to make decisions. She likes and wears mostly pastel colors. I'm...well...I'm the opposite."

"And does Lily ever visit you here?"

"No," I said, sadly. "I'm not sure I'd want her to see me here. Like this."

"Is she also homosexual?" His accent made the word sound funny, and I laughed. His eyes narrowed, a subtle warning.

"Uh, no. She likes guys," I said, thinking of Charley.

He sifted through some paperwork and pointed to our home address. "Does she still live here?"

"I don't know." I shrugged. "Our parents were killed late last year." My voice cracked. "I've been kept out of the loop."

"Good, thank you. I've learned quite enough. You may return to your room."

I felt optimistic. He may not have much of a sense of humor, but at least he didn't ejaculate while talking to me. It was most assuredly a step in the right direction.

41

NOW

Pissed off, Rickie stormed into his room, knocked over his desk chair, swept everything on his desk onto the floor, and threw a balled-up hoodie across the room. Seeing one of the pictures he'd drawn a few days ago in biology class—the one with the vines growing from the woman's vagina—he snatched it off the wall and ripped it to pieces.

Breathing heavily, he sat on the side of the bed. If he was going to fix this, he needed a weapon. Running his hands through his hair, he noticed a bat sitting in the corner. Giving it a couple practice swings, he quickly realized it wouldn't get the job done. Pacing, he glanced out the window. A rusty landscaping truck sat on the curb. The bed overflowed with tree branches and weeds, and he could hear a lawnmower engine roaring somewhere in the distance. The cab door had been left open. There, resting on the passenger seat, was exactly what Rickie needed.

A machete.

* * *

"We gonna be long? Ma said I gotta have the car back in time for her to get to work and start her shift," Wheeler said, peering at the dark, desolate highway.

Pulling onto the side of the road, JT looked at the secluded stretch of forest. "This place is as good as any, I guess." Turning the car off, he jumped out and walked to the trunk.

"You sure he's done?" Wheeler said, following.

"Jesus, you sound like an old lady fer Chrissake! Yes, he's done. You saw him." JT opened the trunk. Dwyer was curled inside, groaning and drooling.

Wheeler stepped away from the car, freaked by Dwyer's blank stare.

"I gotta thank you for coming over today, buddy," JT said to Dwyer. "I thought I was going to have to give up a good thing, ya know? My bitch ain't been the same since you and Johnny-boy worked her over. But no worries, right?" He grinned. "Imma make another."

They pulled him out of the trunk and stood him on the grass beside the road.

"Help me cut the ropes," JT said.

Wheeler stood frozen in fear.

"Whatcha standing there for? Don't want your momma to miss her shift at the fucking Dairy Queen, do you?"

Outraged, Wheeler said, "Hey! She's a manager, man!" as he moved to help.

Once he was freed, Dwyer just stood there, blinking slowly. JT slapped him on the back, sending him rolling down the hill. He grunted and growled as he went. A few minutes later, they heard twigs snap as he made his way deeper into the forest.

"Now what?" Wheeler asked.

* * *

"How long are we going to wait here, bro?" Wheeler asked sometime later, boredom causing him to squirm in his seat. "I thought you said we were just going to come here and fucking get—"

"Look," said JT, cutting him off. "We're going to stay here until the right fucking one comes along. All right? Your mom already missed her shift, so we've got all the time in the world." He watched a silver car pull in beside the gas pumps at the Kum & Go. "I ain't going to settle for the first fucking thing that walks by, man."

A woman wearing a bikini top, cut-off jean shorts, and some platform flip-flops got out of the car. Wheeler sat forward in his seat. "Okay," he said, smiling. "Here we go. *Look at that ass.* You see that?"

"Yeah, I see that. I can't fucking miss it. There's enough fucking cottage cheese spilling out of there to feed Ethiopia!"

"No, bro! It ain't that bad at all."

"Ain't that bad ain't good enough. Jesus, Wheeler."

The woman started pumping gas into her car, then entered the Kum & Go. JT could see the cashier poring over a Penthouse magazine through the window.

"Look, man," Wheeler turned to JT, who ignored him. "Hey!" He tapped JT's shoulder until he had his attention. "This might be our only fucking chance, okay? She's the only piece of split tail that has come by in the last hour, all right?" He pointed at the woman, who was standing in the door talking to the cashier...the cashier who was gawking at her breasts. "Look at her jugs, man! Fucking hot, right?"

JT studied her. "True," he said reluctantly.

Wheeler pounded on the dash in excitement. "All right! Look, that's the best we're going to get out here. Let's do it, all right?"

"All right. Fine, fine, fine." JT held up his hand in surrender. "Just wait 'til she comes back out. You know what to do."

As if hearing him, she ended her conversation and strutted across the parking lot toward her car. "I'm going in," Wheeler said. He turned and waved at JT as he made his way toward her.

"Don't look at me, dumbass," JT mumbled, annoyed.

As he watched Wheeler talk to the woman, his movements over-the-top and clownish, JT frowned and rubbed his forehead, mumbling, "I'm really taking a step down, aren't I?"

She finished using the gas pump, then followed Wheeler across the parking lot. JT peered at her as she made her way to the back of the car. She was older than he thought. Wheeler pounded on the hood of the trunk. "Yo, JT! The trunk, bro!"

JT fiddled with his seatbelt, reluctant to get out. "Okay." He exhaled deeply. "Here we go."

"Ain't giving you nothin' 'til I seen it," she said to Wheeler as JT made his way to the trunk.

"Yeah, sure" Wheeler said, eyes widening at JT.

Up close, she was scary…chipped nail polish, hairy legs, rotten-looking teeth, greasy hair, a large roll of fat perched above the waistband of her cut-off shorts. Even her tits looked saggier from this distance.

"And it better be good," she said, her accent pure trailer-trash. "I know good when I see it. So don't be trying to pass off no oregano on me, you little motherfuckers."

"JT, the trunk, buddy."

JT rolled his eyes and apathetically opened it.

"What's wrong with your buddy there?" she asked Wheeler. "He slow or something?" She peered into the trunk. "Well, I don't see nothing."

"Here you go, baby," Wheeler said, swinging a tire iron into her skull. A hollow, metallic thunk echoed through the parking lot.

The woman turned, looking blankly from Wheeler to JT and back to Wheeler again, as blood trickled down her face. Without saying a word, she punched Wheeler, rebreaking his nose and knocking him to the ground.

JT gaped. *This should have been easy! She's just a…*

Anticipating her next move, JT ducked as she swung at him, then tackled her to the ground. Rolling across the blacktop, she somehow got the upper hand, pummeling JT, really pounding the living shit out of him.

What the ever-loving fuck just happened? he wondered, when the blows let up.

Wheeler managed to get up and ran toward her, the tire iron held in his hands like a baseball bat. She twisted, dodging the blow, and punched Wheeler again in his gore-covered nose. His shriek was effeminate as he fell to the ground.

JT and Wheeler lay helplessly on the blacktop, writhing in pain. Wheeler groaned, "Well, that couldn't have gone worse." He coughed up some blood.

A couple quick kicks with her chunky flip-flops to their heads left them incapacitated long enough for her to steal their wallets. "Sons of bitches!" she screamed as she rushed to her car. Opening the door, she added, "Fuck you!" before climbing inside and driving away.

"Fuck, fuck, fuck! Shit!" JT struggled to his feet in agonizing slowness. Wheeler painfully pulled himself up, and they both returned to their car. Sliding into the driver's seat, JT slammed the steering wheel with his hands. "Shit! Fuckin' fuck!"

"You all right?" Wheeler asked, trying to staunch his bleeding nose while also laughing hysterically, as if he'd completely lost his mind. "You okay?"

"Am I okay? No, I'm not okay! Not fucking funny, man!"

Wheeler couldn't stop the laughter. "You wanted a tough bitch. Wasn't she a fuckin' tough bitch?"

"She fucking outweighed us both!"

"No!" Wheeler said, insulted. "Fuck you!"

"I didn't even want her to begin with, you dumb piece of shit."

Something slammed against the hood of their car. "Holy—!" JT started to say.

"*There* you are!" JoAnn Skinner, of all people, shouted. Her expression was determined and more than a little pissed off.

Swallowing hard, JT said, "Hey…JoAnn."

"I want to know what the fuck you did to my boyfriend!" Again, she slammed her hands down on the hood.

"No, you don't," Wheeler said, offering a goofy grin.

"We didn't do nothing," JT said. He started the engine.

JoAnn came around to the driver's side window, tears in her eyes. "Just fucking *tell* me."

After a moment, his expression calculated, JT said, "Why don't we just…show you?"

42

THEN

"I do things a little differently than Dr. Bagshaw." Dr. Gerhard said, holding a syringe in his hand. "I learned a great deal when I lived in Europe. I was…a well-known medical researcher with a focus on women and children." He paused, a gleam in his eye. "And twins. You're very lucky I'm working here, Ivy."

I was no longer getting good, positive impressions from this man.

"This blend is a little something I cooked up to help you with your…shall we say, *alternative* choices?"

"What is it?"

"That does not matter."

"It matters to me. It's my body. My *one and only* body."

"A body which the asylum legally controls." Dr. Gerhard's once charming, gap-toothed grin was hard, mean. "Now bend over."

Intimidated and mildly alarmed, I did as I was told. He pulled my elastic-waisted pants down just enough to expose the fleshy part of my buttock, pulled the skin taut, and plunged the needle into the tender flesh.

"You're dismissed."

"That's it?" I asked, baffled. "That's my entire treatment?"

"Yes. Now go. And remember to report any changes, physical or emotional."

"Uh, sure."

It wasn't until later that night, as I was getting ready for bed, that the aching muscles started. Hoping I hadn't caught one of the many viruses circulating throughout the hospital, I crawled into bed, pulled the covers over my head, and went to sleep.

* * *

The next morning, I was in agony.

"Good lord, child," said Clara, "your temperature is a hundred and four! I'm taking you to the sick bay!"

"My mouth hurts," I said, struggling to swallow.

Glancing at my face, Clara looked disturbed. "I can see why."

It seemed only moments later that I was lying on a gurney, metal light fixtures streaking past my field of vision as Clara and an orderly rushed me to Dr. Will.

"What's going on?" Will asked, looking me over.

"She's febrile, in pain, and a little disoriented."

"What's her temperature?"

"104."

"Our Ivy doesn't do anything halfway!" He smiled reassuringly. "Let's take a look, shall we?"

He did a full examination, looking inside my ears and mouth, shining a light in my eyes, checking my lymph nodes, and listening to my lungs, heart, and belly. He even hooked me up to the electrocardiogram machine, to make sure I hadn't slipped back into SVT.

"Well, your heart is fine, your lungs sound clear, and your belly is moving as it should."

"But?" I said, drooling a little.

"Your face is swollen. The lymph nodes around your jaw are

enlarged on both sides. Your gums are bleeding, and it seems you're excessively salivating."

"Yeah," I said, sheepishly.

"Any of your teeth hurting?"

I swiped my tongue around my mouth. "All of them."

"Probably just a little oral infection. Might be a tiny cut or abrasion in there somehow. It's hard to say. In the meantime, we'll start you on a round of antibiotics, and you should be right as rain within the week. Just get lots of rest and stay hydrated, okay?"

I nodded, then drifted off to sleep.

* * *

"What do you mean, you got antibiotics?" Dr. Gerhard was not happy.

"I was sick. Some sort of mouth infection. Clara took me to the sick bay, and Dr. Will treated it with antibiotics."

"Did I approve this?" He spit out the words.

"Why would I need your approval to treat something completely unrelated to my homosexuality?"

He slammed his hands on the table. "Because it affects my work!"

"Pardon me, Dr. Gerhard, but fuck your work! I refuse to die from some random infection because of your stupid research. I'm not a guinea pig!"

"Oh, but you are." His grin was cold as ice.

That night, I was secretly moved to a damp, dark room somewhere below ground level.

43

NOW

Machete in hand, Rickie crept into the room. White twinkle lights were strung throughout, giving the space a cozy, festive feel. White candles burned inside glass jars, offering an additional warm glow.

Deadgirl was no longer on the gurney. Instead, she'd been tied to one of the metal pipes. Her arms were raised above her head, forcing her to stand. Dark brown hair, oddly shiny and lux for a woman who hadn't eaten or had any fluids since they'd found her, covered her face as her head drooped forward. Rickie's lips quivered as he raised the machete, ready to cut through her neck and end it all.

Then he heard crying. *Human* crying. Craning to see where the sound was coming from, he spotted a swatch of auburn hair. On the opposite side of the pipe—tied, blindfolded, and gagged—was JoAnn Skinner. Rickie raced to her side.

"JoAnn." He removed the gag. Her face was streaked with sweat and tears. "Okay. Okay. It's going to be okay." His eyes nervously scanned the room, double checking, but they were alone.

"Rickie, don't leave me." The words came out strangled as she sobbed.

"I'm going to get you out of here, okay? I'm going to get you out of here." He cut through the rope securing one wrist and started on the other.

"Fuck you!" she screamed as she tore off her blindfold. Her free hand pounded his chest. "Your fucking friends kidnapped me and you...fucking deviants...hurt my boyfriend! What the fuck is wrong with you, Rickie?"

"I wouldn't do anything to hurt you, JoAnn."

She smacked him again. "I fucking stood up for you. I did fucking everything I could to protect you!"

He grabbed her wrist. "Quit fighting me!"

"Fuck you!"

"Just quit fighting me, okay?"

"No!" She struggled.

"Look, I'm here to help you. I'd never hurt you. *Never*."

Exhausted, she leaned her body against his.

"You're here to *what*, Rick?" asked JT, appearing from nowhere.

Shit. The guy can move like a fucking ninja.

Rickie stepped away from JoAnn and pointed the machete at JT, whose face was covered in bruises.

"You're here to, uh, save the damsel in distress?" JT asked. "Be the big hero?" He grinned. "Nah. That can't be. We all know you ain't no hero."

"JT, what the fuck is she doing down here, man?"

JT smiled lazily. "Whaddya think?"

A voice came from behind him. "Deadgirl." It was Wheeler, loops of twinkle lights slung over his shoulders. "We can make more."

"What?" Rickie asked. He looked at JT, full of confusion.

"You remember that conversation we had about superpowers? You were right. Good ol' Deadgirl's got at least one more trick up her sleeve."

Wheeler added, "See, all she's gotta do is take one bite out of you and...wooooo! JT figured it out."

"What the fuck are you talking about?" Rickie hadn't thought they could horrify him any further, but…

"Damn, Rickie. You're supposed to be the brainiac around here. You saw what happened to Johnny. It's just like in the movies." Wheeler started zombie-walking around the room.

JoAnn piped up, her voice shaky. "Look, I don't know what the fuck is going on around here, but it has nothing to do with me."

"Oh, sweetheart." JT smirked. "I think it's got just about *everything* to do with you, doesn't it?"

Overcome, JoAnn wept.

"Over my dead body, JT," Rickie said, staying close to JoAnn.

"Think about it, all right? Folks like us are just cannon fodder for the rest of the world. But down here, you see, we're in control." He and Rickie circled each other, JoAnn and Deadgirl between them. "Now, we call the shots, man. Feels good, doesn't it? It's all right to say so. You don't have to be the nice guy down here, Rickie."

"Yeah, man." Wheeler gave up his zombie-walk and began stringing more twinkle lights. "This is all for you."

"Enough with the goddamned lights already, Wheeler!" JT yelled. He looked back at Rickie. "Even if you did save her, whaddya think she's gonna do? Why, I bet she wouldn't even thank you. And then she'd send us all to jail forever, and you'd never get her *or* anyone else."

Realizing how bad their situation was, Rickie could only shake his head. "JT, please just let her go."

"You sure that's what you want?"

"Please," he whispered.

"Is that *really* what you want?"

Distressed, JoAnn followed their conversation with her eyes.

"She sure is beautiful," JT said.

"Fuck yeah, she is," Wheeler agreed.

"All right, Wheeler, all right! I'm talking to Rickie now, so please shut the fuck up."

Wheeler retreated to the shadows, pouting.

"JT, man…don't fucking make me do this, okay?"

"Look, I get it," JT said. "You don't want to share, and that's understandable. I respect it. You want what should have been yours a long time ago. And that's what I'm trying to do for you. I am doing this for *your* benefit, Rick. She's all yours."

Hearing the words, JoAnn cried louder. Then, as Deadgirl squirmed, lifting her head, her face mottled and grotesque, JoAnn felt the movement through their shared ties. "Wait, who the fuck is that?"

"Don't you worry about her, honey," JT responded.

"JT," Rickie grumbled, fed up.

Craning her neck, JoAnn tried to look behind her. "Who *the fuck* is that?"

44

THEN

"Please...*help me.*" I whispered.

Dr. Gerhard smiled. "I do believe you've reached the gangrenous stage of Noma. Well done!" He pulled my mouth open and shined a light inside. "We've got severe oral necrosis, facial swelling, and some moderate disfigurement. I count at least four ulcerative holes in your cheeks, and you smell absolutely unholy." He chuckled. "I knew you'd be perfect. The conditions in this shithole are as bad as fucking Auschwitz. You are malnourished, unclean, dehydrated, and depressed. The perfect conditions for Noma to grow and destroy tissue."

"What...is...Noma?" I asked, as a mixture of pus, drool, and blood dribbled from my mouth.

"Gangrenous stomatitis," he replied. "Or, in layman's terms, gangrenous mucosa of the mouth. It can also spread to your vaginal mucosa."

"Why...you...doing...this?"

"Because now, you lucky girl, I'm going to inject you with the cure." He drew some dirty looking brown fluid from a vial into a syringe. "I had to let your tissue reach stage three necrosis before I could try this little cocktail of mine. Antibiotics won't work for you now." He grinned at me, his eyes crazy. "You're the first. The very first human ever to be injected with my greatest achievement…something I like to call Nomaricle!"

"Yeah. Lucky…me." The pain was incredible, but at least my sarcasm was still intact.

"Before I inject you, I want to check your genital area. I've noticed a peculiar aroma." He spread my legs apart, the cloth restraints pulling taut against my ankles. Putting on a pair of gloves, he gave me a quick pelvic exam. "Oh, my. your vaginal tissue is sloughing off. And I see boils. Lots of them." He coughed. "Can't stay down here very long. The smell is singeing my nose hair." He roughly palpated my lower abdomen, eyebrows raised.

"Help…me." I asked again, unable to stand anymore examinations. "Please."

"This shot should fix everything, but…"

"But…what?"

"Have you had sexual relations with a man recently?"

I could only stammer, my thoughts racing.

"Not…willingly."

For a moment, genuine sadness crossed his features. And sympathy. It disappeared just as quickly.

"Well, I do believe you're with child. Perhaps three to four months."

The wail that exploded from my throat wasn't human. If I could have curled into a fetal position, I would have, but my arms and legs were tied. How much was I expected to take?

"The medication will likely cause a spontaneous abortion of the fetus." His tone was surprisingly gentle. "If it doesn't, I'll take care of it for you. There may also be some serious unexpected side effects. You're the first person to ever receive this drug." He became more childlike, even gleeful. "We shall see!" He swiped my skin with an alcohol swab and injected the medication into my thigh muscle. "I'll be back first thing in the morning to do an exam. Would you like some water before I go?"

I nodded.

He lifted my head from the mattress and gave me sips through a straw. "Better?"

Drinking hurt, but I was crazed with thirst.

As the hours passed, the pain in my skin ebbed. I cried in gratitude and relief.

Until the contractions started.

45

NOW

"You've got me all wrong, man," Rickie said.

"Do I?" JT kept circling. "No, I'm thinking I know you a little bit better than you even know yourself these days."

"Then you know I'm fucking done with you, man."

"Rickie," JT said, like he was talking to a child. "She is going to send us to jail. Don't you at least want to sample a little of that prime pussy before you go?"

"No."

"You know it's got to be done. Enough with the goddamned machete already, okay?"

Wheeler stepped closer, looking coyly at JoAnn.

"Wheeler, what are you doing?" JT asked, startled.

Rickie pointed the machete at him. "Yeah, *what the fuck* are you doing?"

Wheeler smirked.

"Don't you fucking touch her, man," Rickie warned.

Wheeler ran his finger down the front of her shirt as she cried.

"Don't you fucking touch her, Wheeler, I swear to fucking God!"

"You won't believe it...me and JoAnn Skinner!" Wheeler said, laughing. JoAnn coughed, then gagged.

"She seems thrilled." JT shook his head. "Wheeler, I wouldn't."

Rickie raised the machete as Wheeler walked his fingers down her stomach toward the waistband of her pants. "I said, don't fucking touch her!"

"That's a bad idea, man," JT said, sounding concerned.

"Last warning. Get your fucking hands off her!"

As Wheeler grabbed her breast, Rickie swung the machete.

Something landed on the floor with a meaty thunk.

JoAnn squeezed her eyes shut and screamed.

JT's face reflected abject horror.

Rickie looked stupefied, staring at the machete.

Wheeler lifted his arm, which ended at the wrist. Blood squirted from the amputation. Child-like, he looked at Rickie. "What'd you do that for?" he asked, before collapsing.

46

THEN

"The Noma injections were never meant to cure my lesbianism, were they?"

Dr. Gerhard scoffed. "Of course not. I wanted to finish my research, and you were a perfect candidate."

"Are there others?"

He didn't hesitate. "Yes. But the rest were unable to survive the infection and have gone into the crematorium."

"Is that what I've been smelling?" Nothing shocked me anymore.

"Indeed."

"Did my baby go in there as well?"

He looked at me, considering his response, while stroking his mustache. Deciding to be honest, he said, "Yes."

"Was it a girl or boy?" My voice was emotionless. Monotone.

"It was disfigured. The Noma infection had spread to your womb. I could not determine its gender without dissection, which I opted not to do."

"How are you getting away with this?" I wanted to cry for my mutant child, but I couldn't. If I hoped to survive, I had to focus only on myself.

"Nobody cares. The patients here are nothing more than cattle. If they disappear, the staff shrugs and moves on."

"But, their families…"

"The families don't care either. You're an embarrassment to them. A dirty little secret. But to me, Ivy, you're my magnum opus! You healed beautifully, as if nothing had ever happened! You look younger and more beautiful than before…as if I discovered the Fountain of Youth! It's a miracle there were no further side effects."

"My family cares," I replied, ignoring the comments about his miracle drug. Though my flesh had healed without any left-over traces of the gangrene, I hadn't felt remotely like myself since the moment he injected me. "I know Violet and Lily would never allow these things to happen to me if they knew."

"Au contraire! Violet has been paid handsomely to keep quiet. And what Lily doesn't know won't hurt her."

"Violet…*knows*?" My heart physically hurt. I felt gut-punched. "She knows what you're doing to me?"

"Not only that, but she also feeds me information about your twin. It's so important to have a control subject in scientific research. Wouldn't you agree?"

"Leave Lily out of this!" My scream was violent. "She's too good for this place and far too good for you."

"You don't have much say in the matter, I'm afraid." He pulled out a clipboard and pen. "Which leads me to our next topic of discussion. Looking at Dr. Bagshaw's notes, it seems no combination of therapy or procedures have helped with the homosexuality issue." He paused dramatically. "So, tomorrow, I endeavor to fix you once and for all. I have a surgical procedure in mind."

"Surgery?" My voice was small.

"It's simple, really. I'm going to sever all the connections between your frontal lobe and thalamus."

"Brain surgery?" Tears poured down my cheeks.

"Yes and no. I don't have to drill into your skull. It's a transorbital procedure. I'll go in through the eye socket instead," he said, placing his clipboard on my bed.

"Oh my God," I said, intentionally covering it with my legs. "Please reconsider."

"*Nein*. I will not. I will be back tomorrow afternoon to perform the procedure. Good night."

"Dr. Gerhard?" I called out.

He paused at the door just long enough to glance back. "Yes?"

"Clara?" I pleaded.

He thought for a moment. "Very well. I'll send her in the morning. Now get some sleep. Tomorrow is a big day!"

I cried quietly, as the flame on the lone candle danced and sparked.

47

NOW

"Well, you sure picked a pretty shit-poor time to man up, Rick," JT said, his voice raspy and nervous. "Who you trying to be, anyway, man? Since day one, it's been you and me. JT and Rickie all the way. And we don't...change. We don't have to, because it's us, man. Rickie and JT. Nothing's got to change between us. Nobody's got to change, you know? It's just you and me, right?"

Rickie watched him closely, the machete ready.

"JoAnn Skinner, man? You think *she's* going to choose *you* in the real world?"

JoAnn gazed at Rickie with big green eyes and mouthed, "*Please*," through her tears. Her free hand was out of view, and he thought she might be trying to stealthily work at the restraints.

"In the real world," JT went on, "she'd rather die than be with you."

"Yeah...I know," Rickie said, his voice low and tortured.

"So, be reasonable, man. Put down the blade. Just you and me, right?"

"I'm not feeling so good, man," Wheeler said, sounding like he might puke.

"He cut off your fucking hand, man," JT said indifferently, motioning to the severed appendage.

"I'm not...I'm not feeling too good," Wheeler said again, crying and rolling on the floor.

While JT was distracted by Wheeler, JoAnn didn't even try to be subtle. She yanked the restraints loose...not hers, but Deadgirl's.

Screaming and growling, Deadgirl flung herself at Wheeler's prone form.

48

THEN

Dearest Tiger,

I miss you. Every single minute of every single day, I miss you. It would be selfish for me to wish you were here…I would hate that worse than I hate it for myself. But seeing you would certainly brighten the many dark corners of my life. Wherever you are, my sweet sister, I hope you're happy and living the life we always dreamed we'd have as we snuggled in our bed late at night, whispering about the future, and giggling like only sisters can.

I don't know how much time I have. I'm about to lose the light, so I need to say this quickly and without distraction. I'm so sorry for putting the weight of my existence here in this hospital on your shoulders, but I feel I no longer have a choice. They've done awful things to me, Lily. Things I don't wish to speak of ever again, and of which you do not need to be privy. I refuse to pollute your mind. These things… they've changed me in undefinable ways, though not in the ways they'd hoped. (I'm still very much a lesbian, much to their chagrin.)

Tomorrow, I suspect, will be the worst I've endured. I don't really understand what he's doing, this Dr. Gerhard, but I have a strong feeling this surgical procedure will be the end of me. Maybe not physically, though that's a possibility too, but emotionally. That undefinable little spark that makes me…me…might be snuffed out. But, Lily…I don't want to be anyone else. I like me. I like being Ivy Elizabeth Reyes. I like being your twin sister...the crazy, outgoing one, who is too impulsive for her own good. I liked loving Carrie...

Living life boldly has always been important to me. You know that. A life of pain so sharp it cuts like a knife, is not any kind of life I'd choose to live. If the Ivy Reyes you know and love doesn't exist anymore, I'd rather be with Momma, wherever she is.

When I'm discharged, Lily, if you see I'm suffering and unable to do anything about it myself, please do the right thing. Don't let these monsters win. I know I don't have the right to do this, but I'm begging you...just let me rest.

I love you more than myself, Lily, and I hope you love me enough to grant this one request.

I'm so scared.

Love,

Poison

I'd written the letter on the back of Dr. Gerhard's physician's notes. When I'd finished, I put his pen back under the clip and threw the board under my bed. Folding the letter, I placed it beneath my buttocks, figuring the good doctor wouldn't look there. Then I waited for Clara.

Please let Clara come. Please...

* * *

"Oh, my God in heaven, thank you for keeping her alive!"

I startled awake upon hearing Clara's voice. She pushed a cart with a lantern, a wash bucket full of steaming, soapy water, a thick pile of towels, a toothbrush and toothpaste, a hairbrush, and, the very best part, a thick, flaky biscuit with strawberry jam and a tall glass of milk.

"Clara!" I said, blubbering. "I'm so glad to see you!"

"Girl, I thought you was dead, the way you up and disappeared. I've been mourning you for weeks!"

"Is Gerhard here?"

"He's upstairs seeing some other patients. But he sent his whipping boy to guard the door, so let's get going before he decides to crash our party." She unfastened the restraints on my wrists and ankles.

Finally free, I grabbed the biscuit from the cart and hungrily stuffed a chunk inside my mouth…then immediately spit it back out. It tasted awful. I tried the milk…also spoiled.

"I think something's wrong with the food. It's really nasty."

Clara sampled both, then looked worriedly at me. "They taste fine, honey."

"Oh." I didn't know what else to say.

"You look good, though" Clara said, studying me. "At least Gerhard's been feeding you. You got your curves back, and your arms are the same size again!"

Confused, I said, "I haven't eaten since they brought me down here. I get water most days, but that's it."

Clara's face paled. "That can't be. Why, you've been down here for three months, Ivy."

"Three…three months?" I stammered, shocked.

"More like three and a half."

"I haven't eaten, I swear." Shrugging, I said, "But it doesn't matter." I grabbed the letter from beneath me and handed it to her, whispering urgently. "Tuck this into your bra, and as soon as you leave work, take it to the post office. Please, Clara. I'm begging you. I don't have an envelope, but I jotted the address on the back of the letter. It's for Lily, if she's even still living there. Can you do this for me?"

"I have a break coming right after I get you cleaned up, so I'll walk it over to the post office then. It's only a half-mile away, from the main road. I'm happy to."

I couldn't help myself. I cried. "Thank you. You don't know what this means to me. Thank you so much, Clara."

"You don't need to thank me. I'd do anything for you, Ivy."

She pushed my hair away from my tear-stained face, and asked, "What's he doing to you?"

"I...I don't know. He's planning something about my frontal lobe and my eye. I don't under—"

Clara gasped.

"What?"

"A lobotomy?" Her face grew even paler. She looked like she was going to pass out.

"Is that what it's called?"

49

NOW

Deadgirl sunk her teeth into Wheeler's leg.

"Oh, shit!" JT screamed.

"Jesus," Rickie said, jumping back.

Chunks of flesh flew through the air, as Deadgirl savagely ripped at his body with her teeth. "Help me!" Wheeler begged, pitifully.

Rickie ran to JoAnn, freeing her. As they fled from the room, JT called, "Rickie! Rickie! I need you, man!"

Quickly realizing Rickie was only worried about saving JoAnn, JT picked up the machete and looked at Wheeler regretfully.

"I'm sorry, my man, but she bit you." His voice was high, panicked. "This ain't my fault. I'm sorry, but I got to, Wheeler. I got to."

"JT!" Wheeler shrieked.

JT swung the machete.

* * *

Rickie and JoAnn heard the screams from the hallway.

"Oh my God. Oh my God. Oh my God," JoAnn repeatedly whispered.

Grabbing her shoulder, Rickie gave her a gentle push. "Go to the end of the hall!"

"Stay the hell away from me! And don't touch me!" She pulled away from his hand and ran down the corridor.

Rickie followed. "Dammit, JoAnn, I know this place. Left! Go left!"

She took his suggestion but didn't wait for him. "Fuck you, Rickie!"

He watched her cross through a dark doorway, the door wedged half-open. Squeezing through the same gap, he tried to push it completely shut, but it wouldn't budge. JoAnn ran up the stairs that led to the basement level, Rickie right on her heels. When she reached the closed door at the top, she tried to open it…but there was no handle.

Panicked, she pounded on it. "Help! Somebody help!"

"Calm down!" Rickie said, pushing her out of the way and attempting to force the door.

"This door is always open. Not sure why it's closed now." Putting his full weight into it, he rammed it with his shoulder.

"No!" JoAnn pounded it with her fists. "Somebody help me! Help! *Please.*"

Rickie grabbed her. "*No.* Stop it. You need to calm down, JoAnn."

"Get off me!" She slapped him.

"It's not going to open!"

Ignoring him, she attacked the door again. "Please, just please help me…please." She broke into tears.

"It's not going to fucking open!" Rickie said, helping her sit on the top step. "Just calm down, okay. Calm down!"

He sat beside her, breathing heavily.

She slid as far away from him as she could get, her body pushed against the wall. "Don't ever touch me again, you fucking piece of shit! I can't believe I ever considered…"

"Considered what, huh?" He smacked a fist on the wall. "And why the fuck don't you ever fucking listen to me? I try to fucking be good to you! Could you maybe just fucking try listening to me for one second, JoAnn? Just fucking pay attention to me for once? Please? *Fuck!*" Then sobs overwhelmed him. Leaning against her shoulder, he cried. "Fuck." He sniffled. "Shit, I'm sorry. I'm sorry."

She refused to look at him. Her body remained stiff, unmoving.

Grasping her shoulders, he turned her to face him, gently tucking her hair behind her ears. "I'm so fucking sorry, okay? I'm sorry. But it's okay. All right? I'm gonna get you out of here. I promise. I promise—"

Below them, Deadgirl burst through the half-opened door.

50

THEN

"Good afternoon!" Dr. Gerhard said briskly. His accent seemed thicker than usual. "All set? Looks like Clara did a good job getting you properly groomed."

"Yes," I said, so nervous I felt like throwing up.

He turned somber. "Speaking of Clara, I'm afraid I have a bit of bad news."

"I just saw her an hour ago."

"Yes, well, apparently, she had an errand of some sort to run on her lunch break. And, unfortunately, on her way back, she was hit by a car. We were just notified by the police."

"But..."

"I'm afraid she's passed away." He began setting up his surgical instruments. One looked just like an ice pick. A very sharp ice pick. Another like a mallet. "But, as I always say... what's done is done. Get yourself into a good mind space. We want this to be successful, don't we?"

I was too shocked to cry. Too heartbroken to respond. Poor Clara. What would her family do without her?

"She was just a nurse," he said blithely, seeing my distress. "Time to move on."

Had Clara not been forced to put my restraints back on by the guard outside the door, I would have leapt up and killed the German son-of-a-bitch. It was my fault she died. *Mine.* I just hoped she didn't die in vain…that she'd been able to mail my letter to Lily.

"I'm going to give you a quick jolt of electricity to knock you out," he said, putting electrodes on my temples. He bent over, inches from my face, and grinned. "See you on the flip side, as they say."

My body spasmed and seized from the electricity, which rendered me speechless…yet I was still awake, alert.

I watched helplessly as Dr. Gerhard picked up the ice pick and brought it toward my eye. The pain was exquisite as he pushed it into my inner tear duct. My eye steadily watered— whether tears or blood, I didn't know—and my vision blurred. My head sank deeply into the mattress from the force of the mallet pounding against the ice pick. The pressure was so intense, I thought my eyeball would pop from its socket. I heard something crack. It felt as if my head was splitting in two. I wondered if the cracking sound was audible to Gerhard, or if I was only hearing it from inside. Either way, it was horrifying. My head was broken.

Then came a burning, tearing sensation that was horrifically unpleasant. Unendurable.

As Dr. Gerhard continued lightly tapping the ice pick with the mallet, random images flashed through my mind: a lone candle's orange flame, a bathtub filled with dirty ice, olive green floor tiles stained with flaky blood, a cigar sitting in an ashtray, smoke billowing from its tip, a tiny plant growing through a crack in the concrete…hardy and strong.

The plant. The tough little plant, enduring no matter what. A survivor.

And then…it was all gone. What had once been full of vibrant color and life, was now black with squiggles of gray.

The pressure inside my head eased. The fear was gone…but so was everything else.

If I ever saw Dr. Gerhard again…I didn't recognize him.

51

NOW

Rickie pushed JoAnn behind him into the corner of the stairway landing. Trying once again to get the door open, he screamed, "Fuck! Fuck!"

Deadgirl shrieked and clawed, snarling up at them with animalistic hunger.

A length of chain wrapped around her neck from behind, and JT yanked her backward, restraining her. He shouted at Rickie, "You son of a bitch! You fucker! This is your fucking fault! Poor fucking Wheeler. He begged me not to do it, but I couldn't have my fucking friend…"

Deadgirl whirled on him, lunged, and they fell out of sight.

"It's okay. It's okay," Rickie told JoAnn "Hang on, okay? I'll be right back. There might be another way out, so please just hold on."

JT shrieked. Rickie ran down the stairs to a short hallway and tried opening a door at the end. It was locked.

"Goddammit!" He pounded it in frustration. When he returned, JoAnn was gone from the landing. "Shit!" Distressed, he ran his fingers through his hair. "Fuck!"

Through the half-opened door below, he could hear

Deadgirl's inhuman growls and screeches. Knowing it was the only other place JoAnn could be, he rushed in.

The first thing he saw was JT being thrown against the wall by Deadgirl, utilizing the same chain he'd used on her. The impact was so brutal, Rickie wondered if she had broken his spine. JT slid to the floor, back against the wall, eyes wide open.

Deadgirl pounced. She tore into his face with her teeth.

JT wailed. His arms reached out, a cry for help, but all Rickie could do was stand there. Frozen. Eyes bulging.

Not JT. JT is invincible.

Deadgirl spun, hunched like a wild animal, teeth bared. Her skin, the little he could see of it through the blood, remained grotesquely mottled. Viscous blood and chunks of tissue oozed from her mouth. She growled, she screeched, she snarled, she screamed, she moaned, she cried…the sounds alien, unearthly.

Knowing he had nowhere to escape, Rickie just stood there. Watching. Listening. She didn't move, just kept making those hideous noises, her eyes never leaving his face. Rickie couldn't help wondering if she was somehow…someway…trying to communicate.

Then she ran at him, a war-cry-like shriek echoing through the underground chamber. A deer caught in headlights, Rickie couldn't move. She barreled into him, knocking him backward, and bolted through the doorway. Flat on his back, he craned his neck and watched her scramble up the staircase. She ripped the door from its hinges and fled the prison where she'd been held captive for far too long.

Dazed and out of breath, he avoided looking in JT's direction. Rickie knew he was still alive, because he kept choking but didn't try to speak.

He found JoAnn in an alcove. Her expression was blank, skin nearly translucent. He smiled in relief, happy she was okay, not caring that JT was almost certainly right—she would tell the police everything.

"Oh, JoAnn. Thank God."

She tottered unsteadily toward him. Blood dripped on the cement between her bare feet. Rickie's expression changed from joyful to horrified as she started to collapse. Catching her and easing her gently to the ground, he examined her and found a deep wound in her back.

"He...stabbed...me," she said weakly. Then she closed her eyes and went still.

He could see that she was breathing, barely, but had no idea how much time she might have left.

"Rickie..." JT coughed, gagging on thick blood. His entire upper lip had been chewed off. "Oh, God."

"What the fuck, JT? Why would you do this, man? Why?"

JT hitched a shoulder in a version of a shrug.

His mutilated face crumpled as he started crying. "Shit!" He tried to touch the gaping hole where his lip used to be but couldn't. "I know it got outta hand. I was just trying to help, Rickie. I did it for you."

"No, you did it for *you*. I kept giving you the benefit of the doubt, and you kept disappointing me. I thought you were my friend."

"I am," he whispered, smiling weakly.

Stroking JoAnn's auburn locks, Rickie said to her, "Hold still and breathe. I'm gonna get you outta here, okay? Just hold on." Holding back tears, he looked blankly around the room, trying to figure out what to do. "Breathe, JoAnn. It will be okay, I promise."

"Just don't tell my grandma, huh?" JT asked, as blood and copious amounts of saliva ran down his chin.

Rickie pulled JoAnn's prone form across the floor, smearing streaks of crimson.

Snot ran from JT's nose. "Rickie? I can already feel it inside me. Fuck."

JoAnn moaned.

"Don't worry. I'm not going to let you..." Rickie couldn't say the word. "I'm going to get you out of here. It will be all right."

JT watched them, despair etched across his face.

Resting at the bottom of the stairs, Rickie cradled JoAnn's head. "Can you hear me? Just hold on for me. I won't let you...*d..die*...JoAnn." He stumbled over the word. "I won't let you die."

Eyes unable to focus, JoAnn mumbled, "What did you say?"

"I said that I love you," Rickie replied, caressing her jaw. "I love you, JoAnn...so much."

"Rickie?" JT said, his voice gravelly. "I can still bite her before it's too late."

Ignoring JT, Rickie focused his entire attention on the girl in his arms. He leaned down, inches from her face. "Listen, I love you. I do. I've loved you for so long. I'm in love with you, JoAnn."

JoAnn coughed, then spit a wad of blood in his face. "Fucking grow up," she said, her voice raspy. "Just take me home, Rickie."

Gasping in shock, feeling kicked in the gut, Rickie released her. Leaning back against the wall, his hand trembled as he pulled at his hair, trying to wrap his head around a very new reality.

She didn't love him. She didn't even like him. She never would.

JoAnn coughed, her breaths labored. Blood trickled from her mouth. "Take...me...home ...Rickie...please."

Rickie looked at JT, barely hanging on, drool running down his chin from a deep, otherworldly hunger.

A sob escaped him. He couldn't lose the two people he loved most.

"Please," JoAnn begged. "Please help me."

52

THEN AND NOW

It's so dark. I can only hear drips from leaking pipes. Why is there plastic draped over me? Is this somebody's idea of a joke? I'm so tired...

A rat is sitting on my chest. The weirdest thing...I really want to eat him. Lily would be horrified.

My legs keep moving as though I'm running. Running through the rows of the vineyard. Picking juicy grapes and popping them into my mouth. No, wait. The thought of food makes me feel sick. Oh, well. Surely, I'll be discharged soon.

I wonder where Dr. Gerhard is. I could use a sip of water. And why haven't I seen Clara for a while? Maybe she just doesn't like me anymore. I am sad.

I wish I could roll over.

Two boys are here. Are they taking me home? Why are they arguing? One has kind eyes. They remind me of Lily's eyes. I hope he'll be my friend.

Why is the other one trying to hurt me? My face. My neck. Oh, no. No, no, no, no! Please don't do that down there again. Please, no...

So this is what it feels like to be shot. Not my favorite. I wish I knew why this boy keeps trying to kill me. I'm just a young girl.

His hand is so soft and warm. I like him. I think Lily would too. Maybe we can be friends. I hope he takes me home to my family.

I can move my hand. Maybe I will teach these mean boys a lesson.

Please don't put it in there! Are you crazy? Those are bullet holes!

I can't stop gagging. Why is he pushing it down my throat? It tastes dirty, sweaty. I don't like it. But what if…

He sure is screaming a lot, when I'm the one whose face is battered. But his blood…it's delicious.

This guy sure doesn't know much about make-up.

Ooh! The twinkling lights are pretty!

I told the boy with the nice eyes thank you as I ran out of the build-ing. I hope he understood. Fuck the rest of them.

It is dark as I run through the forest. I don't know where I am or what year it is…I'm not even sure who I am anymore. I just know where I'm going. Images of succulent, juicy purple grapes flash through my mind.

I come to a small creek. Delighted, I jump in, washing the blood and grime from my body. The icy water feels wonderful against my battered skin as I splash and play. I laugh, but it sounds like a grunt. Oh well, I am free!

A large fish swims by, and I grab it, biting into its iridescent scales. Momentarily satiated, I run along the creek bed until I hear voices. Hiding behind a tree, I listen to a young couple chatting as they put out their campfire.

"Did you hang your damp clothes on the line?"

"Yep. Yours too."

"Thanks, babe. Sure would be nice to have a washer and dryer in the camper."

"The whole purpose of camping is to *not* do those kinds of chores. You need to learn to enjoy the peace and quiet of nature, Meg."

The woman stands up. "I'm going inside. It feels like a

movie and ice cream kinda night." She pauses in the doorway. "Want to join me?"

Rolling his eyes, the man pours water over the remaining embers. "Not exactly enjoying nature," he grumbles, but follows her inside.

I look at the garments swaying in the breeze.

Clothes. Do I need them?

Deciding I probably do, I blindly grab a couple things off the line and carry them back into the woods. The jeans are far too long, but I roll them up, proud of myself for remembering how. The woman's t-shirt is on the baggier side and has the letters R.E.M. on the front. I have no idea what that is, or why a woman would wear such a baggy shirt, but it serves the purpose. Satisfied that I am appropriately attired, I venture on, trusting my innate instincts. I walk for miles. Sometimes, I even hum.

Although I don't need to sleep, when the sun rises, I find a dense canopy of trees and rest on the thick grass beneath. Though I'm not sure why, I know it will be unsafe if I am found.

All day, faces and images play in my mind, like a movie with no dialogue—

A large tree beside a grand home. A cute girl with thick, brown hair and an upturned nose. A syringe filled with murky fluid. A tan blonde. A man with a gap-toothed smile. A round, elderly woman. Barrels...so many barrels. A boy with floppy hair and kind eyes. A small, unattractive penis...

When the sun sets, I resume my journey.

* * *

Day by day, I make my way north, feeling an urgency to get where I am going, though I don't understand why. I maintain my routine of walking only at night and resting during the day, staying in wooded areas or on rarely traveled roads. The closer I get to my destination, the colder the nights become. I sneak into a cabin I come across deep in the woods and pilfer a warm jacket, a pair of socks, and some too-large boots. I pack them with leaves, so they won't fall off my feet.

When I get lost, I sniff the air, the scents drifting on the breeze telling me which way I need to go. Eventually, the terrain starts to become familiar. While some of the homes look the same, most don't. And are those *cars*?

It is difficult to stay concealed, because this town—I somehow know—is way busier and more populated than it was. As I make my way up a long driveway under a canopy of stars in a navy sky, I see a black metal archway over the road: REYES WINERY.

Just like that, I remember.

* * *

My childhood home looks the same, yet different. But I recognize it as my own. I walk around the side where I know I'll find a tree. And a second-story window.

Lily.

The house is dark, but the front door light is on, as always. I knock. "Hello!" I try to call, but a creepy moan is all that comes out. After several minutes, an eye peeks through a crack in the chained door.

"Yes? Can I help you?" says a feeble female voice. She sounds scared.

I peer into the crack, trying to smile, and hear the woman draw in a sharp breath.

"Poison?" she whispers in disbelief.

* * *

The quick rattle of a chain, and the door is yanked open. An elderly woman in a flannel nightgown stands in the entryway, shorter than me, with white hair and kind brown eyes.

"Is it you?" she whispers, then shakes her head as though trying to clear it. "No, of course it's not you. But you must be related. Are you Ivy's granddaughter?"

I can't respond. I can only stand there staring at this woman who looks vaguely familiar, but who smells *very* familiar. Thinking it might help, I show her my faded wrist tattoo.

She gasps, covering her mouth with her hand.

"Ivy!" She stares at me incredulously. "But...how have you not aged? Where have you been? What happened? And who hurt you?" Pulling me inside the house, she says, "It's me, Ivy. It's Lily!" She shows me her own tattoo, wrinkled and ugly on thin, veiny skin.

My legs weaken, and I slide to the ground. Lily is my twin, but this woman looks nothing like me. I don't understand.

Helping me up, she ushers me to a plush sofa. I study my surroundings. I remember this room. It's the same room where Daddy broke my arm. Thinking of him, I look at his swords still displayed over the fireplace and frown.

Handing me a glass of iced tea, Lily sits beside me. "Can you speak?"

I shake my head.

I can only gaze at her.

"I still don't understand everything," she says, rubbing her forehead. "All I know is, Daddy and Momma dropped you off at that awful place and then came home. Daddy seemed happier than ever, but it hit Momma hard. She told me how horrendous it all seemed and how guilty she felt for leaving you there by yourself. Daddy somehow convinced her it was for the best, but she was never the same after that. Daddy never gave us updates, either, though I now know he was receiving them."

She sips her own tea as she talks. Though we're reunited at last, she seems so nervous. Surely, she's not scared of me...her own sister, her twin?

"We didn't know what was happening or when you'd be home. Then they...they were killed in a car accident. Daddy was drunk. It was a head-on collision. Daddy flew through the windshield. He was dead on impact. Momma was crushed inside the car." Lily chokes up. "She was...decapitated, Ivy."

I place my hand on her arm. She flinches but tries to pretend it didn't happen as she continues speaking.

"Robert was still alive when they found him, but the trauma was too much, and he died at the hospital." She drew a deep, shaky breath. "We buried them in the family plot. Violet inherited everything, including this house. I moved in with Charley, and we were married the following year." A thin smile manages to curve her lips. "We have four children, ten grandchildren, and two great-grandchildren." Then the smile fades. "Charley died a few years ago. Heart attack. Our children are spread out across the country. I'm here alone now, I'm afraid."

She refills her teacup. "Would you like more?" she asks before realizing I haven't taken a single sip.

I cannot reply, can only continue listening. "Violet swore she knew nothing regarding you or your whereabouts. It was a lie, of course. The doctors had been in contact with her, even paid her for information. About us...about me. I discovered it all when Violet died." She pauses, thinking. "I guess it's been thirty-five years ago now. Cancer. Ovarian, I believe. Her death was long and excruciating. She was only forty-seven. Never married. I couldn't help but think karma might have played a part."

She gives me an encouraging look, which I try to return, though it is hard for me to keep up. Memories of Violet gradually return.

Though she's trying hard to cover it, Lily is very uncomfortable around me. Twins shouldn't make each other nervous. I wish we could pick up where we left off. It isn't fair. I finally find her, and she's scared of me.

"She knew where you were and what they were doing to you all along, but I didn't. Not until after she died, when I went through the paperwork. Charley and I and...Carrie...drove down to Evansburgh, hoping to pull you out of that awful place, but it was closed. It closed permanently in 1947. The building had been condemned. We went to the library and did some research. We found out about Dr. Gerhard, and his...experiments." She shudders, looking deeply sorrowful, as she wraps her arms around me. It feels nice. "I'm so utterly sorry I failed you."

I must have perked up when she'd mentioned Carrie's name, and she'd noticed.

Continuing, she says, "Carrie lives in New York City. She's an actress. Was on Broadway. Never married. Never stopped looking for you." Lily clears her throat, takes another drink of tea.

Memories of Carrie are both clearer and sweeter than those of Violet.

"And that...that Dr. Gerhard," Lily continues with difficulty, "it turns out, was a Nazi war criminal. His real name was Josef Mengele. Yes, Mengele! They tracked him down, knew he worked in your hospital. But before they could catch him, he fled to South America. They say he hid out there until he died. In 1979, I think it was."

1979...the numbers seem incomprehensible, and it must show on my face.

"Oh," Lily says softly, as if realizing something. "Do you...do you even know what year it is?"

I moan.

"It's 2008," she says, quietly.

Those numbers are even less comprehensible.

"It's been almost sixty-three years since you were committed. We'll be eighty next month. Eighty—"

I throw the mug of tea across the room in a fit of rage. It shatters against the stone fireplace. Animalistic wails rise from deep inside my chest.

My entire life...

Decades. I spent decades alone inside a condemned building.

"Were you there, in that hospital, the whole time? Even after they closed it? The patients were supposedly transferred to other facilities. At first, we assumed that's what happened to you, but there was no record. Then, when we learned about the crematorium, I thought you must've died. All this time, Ivy, I thought you were dead. I couldn't feel you anymore…not in my head, or in my heart." Tears run down her cheeks. "I'm just so damn sorry I didn't do more. But how is this even possible? How did you survive?"

I shrug.

We sit in silence for a few moments, then Lily stirs.

"I have a few things to show you," she says. "Wait here." She hobbles out of the room and returns with a box. "Do you remember the day you went through Momma's jewelry? You mentioned wanting pretty, sparkly jewelry when you were older, so I saved this just for you."

She opens the box. Inside is a beautiful ruby and diamond necklace with matching bracelet.

"May I put them on you?" she asks.

I nod and she gently places them around my bruised neck and wrist. I make my way to the hallway mirror. I preen. I don't see the monster I've become, but the sixteen-year-old girl I was.

Lily's eyes are misty as she watches me. "Red always did suit you. You look so beautiful. Just like you did all those years ago!"

She's being so nice to me. Maybe everything will be all right.

Producing a folded sheet of yellowed paper, she says, "I also found this in Violet's things. It's the letter you wrote to me."

I grab it out of her hand, staring at writing I can no longer read.

"I didn't even see it until *twenty-six years* later. Violet never told me a thing." Her voice turns sad. "The lobotomy that horrible man did on you…I sometimes wondered if that's why I couldn't feel you with me anymore."

Not wanting to talk any further about this, I move down the

hall, to the staircase. Looking up from the bottom, I can see into Robert's old bedroom, which is now an office. I hear Lily behind me—did she just choke back a sob?—as I trudge slowly up the steps.

Stairs no longer feel easy or normal for me. I want to crawl up, but I know I need to behave as normally as possible.

At the top, I turn right. Our room is at the far end of the hall.

Pushing open the door, the first thing I notice is how nothing much has changed. A small bedside lamp shines brightly in the otherwise dark room. There is the same white iron radiator. There is the same rocking chair in the corner. There is the same yellow and lavender quilt.

I kneel behind the rocking chair and lift the loose floorboard. My hiding place is still there, but the diary that once filled the space is now likely ashes inside the asylum's crematorium. I never saw it again after I was moved underground.

A sudden sharpness cleaves into my neck. Blood spills down my body, pooling on the hardwood, and dripping onto the cobwebs that stretch across my hiding place.

"Oh my God," I hear Lily sob. "I'm sorry, Poison, so sorry!"

One of Daddy's antique swords, which is displayed above the fireplace, is lodged in my cervical spine.

I am numb with shock and anger.

Lily backs away in horror. "I don't have the strength to do it right."

Why would Lily do this to me?

"...trying to honor your request..." Lily breaks down weeping.

Her words evoke another memory. The letter. I can see my hands forming the words on the paper:

> *'When I'm discharged, Lily, if you see I'm suffering and unable to do anything about it myself, please do the right thing. Don't let these monsters win. I know I don't have the right to do this, but I'm begging you...just let me rest.'*

She is only doing what Lily has always done. She is helping me, just as I'd asked her to.

I've always loved my sister more than anything. We'd shared a womb. We'd shared our looks. We'd shared a life.

And now, we'd share in my death.

I embrace her, giving her the best hug I'm capable of giving, and sink to my knees before her in what was once our childhood bedroom.

I point to the sword in her frail, shaking hands, and bow my head.

"I love you, Ivy," she whispers.

Seconds later, I finally find peace.

53

NOW

Rickie smiled brightly as he walked across the bridge. It was a beautiful day, sunny with cloudless blue skies. Perfect weather for a nice after-school stroll. Graduation was just a few weeks away, and he couldn't wait. School was better these days, but he was ready to move on. He'd already registered at a local community college that offered a variety of summer art classes.

Mostly, he kept to himself. Like today during lunch. He'd read a comic book beneath a big oak tree in the school yard, watching as the new quarterback and his cheerleader girlfriend made out on the bleachers. Some things never changed.

But some things did.

Johnny and Dwyer were now in a long-term care facility, the doctors still baffled by their peculiar symptoms. Dwyer had been found wondering the streets of Evansburgh a couple days after Deadgirl escaped. Worried, Rickie had dropped an anonymous letter into the mail, warning doctors to avoid getting bitten. Whether it worked or not, he had no way of knowing, but he certainly wasn't interested in living through a zombie apocalypse. Though, he'd never considered Deadgirl a zombie. Feral, yes. Animalistic, yes. Zombie? Not even a little. She was so much more than mobile rotting meat desperate for brains. He knew she could feel scared and experience pain, and that simple human touch made her happy. He'd seen it in her eyes...the heart, the soul.

Both Wheeler and JoAnn had officially been declared missing persons, which was just fine by Rickie...but nobody ever mentioned JT. Rickie suspected nobody had noticed he was gone, not even his senile grandma.

Life was slow and drama-free. He went to school, came home after dark, did his homework, and went to bed. His mom had finally kicked Clint out, and Rickie's relationship with her was better than ever.

Standing outside the walls of the Linda Vista Lunatic Asylum, he grinned in anticipation, admiring the intricate architecture of the condemned building that had become his second home.

Once inside, he descended to the basement, then to the sub-basement, where Deadgirl had torn out the door and escaped.

Rickie often wondered what had happened to her. He hoped, wherever she was, that she'd found peace.

Before entering his room, he took a short detour to a small chamber about fifty feet away. Pushing open the door, he grabbed a sealed glass container from his backpack. The smell wafted through the space after he removed the lid, and chains rattled as something drug itself across the floor.

"Here you go, JT. A nice, bloody steak. Enjoy, man." Rickie tossed the meat on the ground.

JT, a metal collar circling his neck that attached to a chain, attacked the meat with gusto. His missing upper lip didn't affect his eating habits. When he finished, he growled at Rickie.

"Yeah, yeah. I didn't forget. Did you think I would?" Rickie placed the latest edition of *Playboy* on the floor, along with a pack of JT's preferred cigarette brand, then backed out of the room. "See ya tomorrow, man!"

JT ignored him as he flipped frantically through the pages of the magazine.

Unlocking the door to his room, Rickie stepped inside. The white twinkle lights still radiated their festive glow, and scented candles masked multiple unsavory odors. The space was clean and tidy. The floors had been scrubbed, the trash cleared. Clothes, mostly white dresses, hung neatly inside a makeshift wardrobe. A new mattress had been placed on the gurney, along with fresh sheets, and a white comforter. Pink flowers sat on the bedside table, along with a wash basin, lotion, perfume, and other feminine essentials. Posters and photos, even some of Rickie's artwork, decorated the space.

The girl lying there was dressed in a white eyelet lace dress with a small bow between her breasts. A gold chain with a pale green pendant circled her neck and rested against her chest. White silk ties wrapped around her wrists and ankles and kept her just where he wanted. Her auburn hair was brushed smooth.

He gazed adoringly at her. "Hi, JoAnn."

Her blank, lifeless green eyes slowly opened.

Q&A WITH TRENT HAAGA

What inspired *Deadgirl*? How did you come up with the title?

I had been working for Troma films and was deeply involved in The Toxic Avenger Part 4 as a writer and producer. We shot it in upstate New York, and there was a long sequence that was supposed to take place in a hospital. Since shooting in a real hospital was not doable, we toured several abandoned mental institutions (and ended up shooting in one). The places were spooky as hell and really atmospheric. Once we finished shooting that film, I had a list of location contacts for abandoned asylums, schools, etc. I love Troma, but my personal taste leans a little weirder and disturbing, so after making an outrageous, gory superhero comedy action movie, I wanted to write something more to my personal taste. So I wrote a script that took place in many of the locations I had contacts for. The plan was to shoot it on digital cameras for super cheap, but Lloyd wasn't interested in making it, so I put it on a shelf for a few years. We ended up shooting it in Los Angeles in 2006, a good six years after I wrote it.

As for the title, I'm a fan of short, punchy titles that are illustrative. DEADGIRL was the essence of this movie stripped down. Also, it was a nod to how this character is dehumanized - she has no name, no designator, no origin ... the boys call her DEADGIRL because to them, that's all she is. Trying to make a title that was provocative, had some meaning, and would grab you when you saw it on the shelf.

Was that *really* Jenny's (Deadgirl's) bush?

Haha! No. That is a common film item called a *merkin* that's created specifically for that purpose - lots of movies with nude scenes use them. It's basically a pubic wig. Also, I believe that Jenny was styled in the way of the Brazilians down there, and to shoot her as-is would have put us in serious NC-17 territory. We were already pushing it with the content anyway, so why have things be more difficult? Also: we felt the character of DEADGIRL wouldn't have much grooming down there...I mean, she's a zombie, right?

How difficult was it working with the dog on set?

The dog only had to work two days, and when you're working with an animal, you just want to get exactly what you need as quickly as possible so that the animal is happy and stays cool. This particular Mexican hairless dog (the breed is called "Xoloitzcuintle") was movie trained and was pretty obedient. I don't remember there being any issues with the dog's performance at all - it was a true professional.

How did you squeeze pus out of the bullet holes in Jenny's abdomen?

Movie magic. It was just a small section of "torso" that our special FX guy, Jim Ojala, created. That way it was easy to manipulate and re-fill. The effect wasn't on Jenny at all - we shot it as an insert. So in essence it was just a tube of torso-shaped latex with a hole we could pump pus through. Editing and sound effects help sell a relatively simple effect.

What was the temp in the room where Jenny had to lay naked?

We shot it in late Spring in Los Angeles, so the weather was nice the whole time and the temperature was just right. Making movies is sweaty work, but we were really in a good place as far as that was concerned. I don't even remember us using air conditioners on set (which must be turned on and off between takes). The weather was super cooperative and nice throughout the shoot, from what I remember.

I've read the draft for the sequel, and it has a very different energy than the first. Tell us a little about your idea for the sequel, and is there any possibility it will be made?

I'm not really interested in sequels as a rule and purposefully make my stories have definitive endings (usually involving everyone dying just to make sure). The distributor of DEADGIRL was interested in a sequel, so I wrote one. I wasn't interested in re-examining the scenarios that I did in the first one, so I went in a totally different direction. A lot of people seemed to think that the first film was misogynistic, which I find odd. it's more misandrist than anything, in my opinion, so I wanted to try a different tact by making the Deadgirl herself the only returning character. What if Deadgirl was just a vessel through which characters could use her to fulfill their twisted fantasies? And what would that fantasy be if a woman were to find her instead of horny teenage boys? What I came up with is something that I liked to pitch as "Precious with an attack zombie."

I'm almost 100% certain that it will never be made, but I like the screenplay, regardless. Hollywood is a crazy place, and you never know what's gonna happen in the future.

What was in the beer cans that Noah (JT) and Shiloh (Rickie) chugged?

Wish that the answer was more exciting, but it was just water.

Were the sex (rape) scenes uncomfortable for the actors/crew?

Movies are so weird. Music and editing and angles give things context and "vibe." But the atmosphere on set is different. We're all in a hurry, trying to do our jobs, and you're NOT shooting a lot more than you are shooting. So while the scenes themselves are quite intense, the atmosphere on set was generally relaxed, and Jenny and the other actors were all on board. They are pros. But a lot of that has to do with Jenny's work ethic and commitment to the material. No one left the set, there were no complaints or weirdness. This movie was made by pros who were all used to making edgy, uncomfortable material in a way that was comfortable for everyone. But I guess you'd have to ask the actors that to get the best answer.

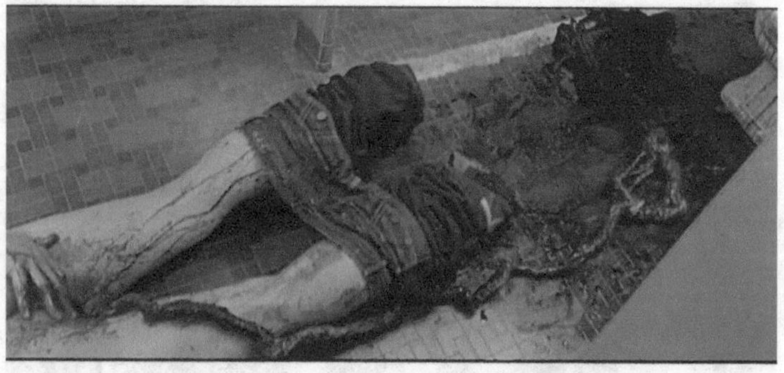

What did you use as intestines in Johnny's infamous bathroom scene?

Jim Ojala to the rescue again. We'd never use real animal guts because of health and safety reasons. Jim whipped up a batch of guts with foam latex and lots of fake blood. Simple as that.

When writing the screenplay, did you have your own backstory for Deadgirl's origins?

Honestly, no. I felt it would take away the mystique of the character and stop her from being the cypher that she was supposed to be. In many ways, the Deadgirl is a *MacGuffin*—a device that furthers the plot. This is fundamentally a morality play with some uncomfortable gender politics in it—the Deadgirl is a thing that comes out of nowhere and interrupts the dynamic and reveals hidden truths. In another movie, she could be a stash of hidden money or a magic locket. So, it was more of what she represented and the effect she has than what she is or where she came from. And people still wonder to this day, so I feel like NOT addressing this made the movie more mysterious and spurred more debate as a result.

Did you have any qualms about handing over your 'baby' to an unknown author for the novelization?

None whatsoever. I already told my story and the fact that someone else wants to play in the sandbox I built is a great indicator that the sandbox I built is valid. Sometimes you make a piece of art, and it just disappears into the ether. It's truly satisfying to know that this thing I dreamt up is now inspiring others to make their own art. It's validating to an extreme, especially considering how hard it was to get the movie made in the first place. No one wanted to do it initially, and now people are volunteering to expand the universe. It's really cool. At the time that I'm answering these questions, I've not read a word of the book you're holding in your hand right now, but I'm certainly looking forward to it and hope to be surprised!

DEADGIRL'S #1 FAN

JEFF STRAND

Stanley smiled as the end credits began for *Deadgirl*. It was his favorite movie by far—nothing else even came close. He'd watched it for the first time when he was a freshman in high school, and now that he was almost done with his junior year, he'd estimate he'd seen it at least a hundred and fifty times all the way through. (Sometimes he just watched the best parts.)

Though it was his favorite movie, it definitely wasn't a perfect movie. He didn't appreciate how the filmmakers seemed to have a disapproving attitude about the events that unfolded. JT, Wheeler, and the others were considered the bad guys, while spoilsport Rickie was the voice of reason, at least until he figured things out at the very end.

Despite the flawed moral stance, which Stanley hoped would be fixed in the novelization, he couldn't get enough of *Deadgirl*. They didn't sell much merchandise for the movie (a huge mistake in his opinion), but he did have the poster on his wall and wore the T-shirt almost every weekend. (His school had deemed it "inappropriate.")

He wanted to recommend the movie to all his friends, but he didn't really have any. Last year, an actual girl, Vicky, had come over so they could work on a biology project together. When they finished, he'd popped in the Blu-Ray and promised she'd really enjoy it. That had been a mistake.

To be clear, Stanley was not a creepy weirdo who spent all his free time in his bedroom, whacking off to the highlights of *Deadgirl*. If anything, his love of the movie got him out of the house!

The term was "urban explorer." People who explored abandoned buildings. Stanley's car was a piece of shit, but it gave him the freedom to travel to all kinds of buildings without relying on rides from his mom, who would have dissuaded him from breaking into private and dangerous properties.

Because this was real life and not a movie, Stanley followed the rule that you left these buildings exactly as you found them...unlike Rickie and JT, who trashed the place for kicks. Stanley was willing to risk getting arrested for trespassing, but he didn't want to add a vandalism charge.

It was a very rewarding hobby.

Lots of fun.

And, no, Stanley was *not* looking for a chained-up naked zombie girl to be his sex slave. That would be utterly ridiculous. The living dead did not exist.

Nor was he looking for a chained-up naked normal girl to be his sex slave. It was preposterous to think that he might just happen to stumble upon one. Even if he went through every abandoned building in America, the chances of finding a naked girl chained to a hospital gurney were almost non-existent. And if he somehow *did* conquer astronomical odds and find one, no doubt her abductor would be right there. Stanley didn't want to fight a serial killer.

Nope. He did not, for one second, believe he would find his own Deadgirl.

It wasn't about believing he would find one. It was about pretending he might find one.

The fantasy was enough.

* * *

The fantasy was no longer enough.

As a senior, Stanley still had no friends. And he never had a girlfriend. But…he went to the same school as Kylie Hawk.

Kylie was reasonably hot, he supposed. She was certainly nobody's idea of a supermodel, but she wasn't unpleasant to look at. Her most noteworthy characteristic, at least to him, was that she was apparently trying to fuck her way through the entire male student body.

Stanley didn't know how she made her selections, whether she started at the top and worked her way down, or if it was based on proximity at any given moment. All he knew was that one afternoon she stopped by his locker and asked if he wanted to hang out after school.

He did. Very much so.

But as they lay naked in her bed, seven minutes after arriving at her house, Stanley could not get hard.

Not at all. Not even a little. Not a tremor of movement.

Kylie, credit where it was due, had done her best. Finally, though, she'd said in a very quiet voice that she didn't think this was going to work out, and that it was time for him to leave. She had to finish an essay for English class.

Stanley silently got dressed, and then slunk out of her house, disappointed to still be a virgin.

What had gone wrong? He'd been nervous but not boner-killing nervous. Kylie's body was perfectly adequate. He hadn't been distracted by thoughts of all the guys she'd been with. So what the hell had ruined his experience?

He figured it out as he drove home: She was too *alive*.

Stanley was not a necrophile. He would never dream of banging a corpse, no matter how physically attractive. That was the realm of complete degenerates, and he hoped they were all locked up for the rest of their deviant lives.

No, he just wanted somebody to behave like...well, like Deadgirl.

He wanted a girl who'd put on some makeup to give her the proper undead complexion, and then let him chain her up. She'd snarl and thrash around, like she was aware of what was happening but too feral to beg for mercy. It wouldn't be rape, of course–it would be entirely consensual, and she'd have a safe word.

He wouldn't beat her up like JT did in the movie.

Unless he found a girl who was into that. He wasn't sure if they existed. He'd watched a few BDSM videos, and there was some choking, but he'd never seen one where the girl let the guy punch her in the face. That was okay. He could probably get hard without it.

He definitely couldn't shoot her. Very disappointing.

The next morning at school, Stanley approached Kylie at her locker. "Would you be willing to give me another chance?"

"Not really, no."

"I was nervous. I won't be nervous this time, I promise."

"Sorry," said Kylie. "It was embarrassing for both of us, and I don't want an encore."

"What if we just watched a movie?"

"I don't want to be rude, but I only barely wanted to fuck you. I certainly don't want to go on a date."

"It's not a date. Just a movie."

"What movie?"

"*Deadgirl.*"

"The one where those dudes rape a zombie?"

"You've seen it?" asked Stanley.

"Yeah. It sucked. I'd rather tug on your tiny, limp dick for ninety minutes than watch it again. Maybe don't talk to me anymore, okay?"

Stanley walked away, trying to put some distance between them before he cried or punched her in the face.

* * *

Clearly, Stanley couldn't approach other girls at his school about his fantasy. Though he didn't care all *that* much about his reputation, it would take only one girl to go around saying, "Can you believe what he asked me?" and his future would be ruined. He didn't care what his bitch of a mother thought—his dad was long gone—but he still wanted to try to get a degree. Even community college admission boards frowned upon that kind of thing.

He supposed a hooker would do it for the right price, but that wasn't in his budget.

Maybe an online ad?

> *Seeking woman into extreme role-play. Light zombie makeup and bondage required. Must be okay with pretending our activities are non-consensual, up to and including intercourse and physical abuse. I'm 17 but can pass for 18 easily. Discretion required.*

Nobody responded.

It seemed like he had two choices: switch from a willing to an unwilling volunteer, or give up on the idea altogether. The latter choice was definitely the smarter one. That was the choice that would keep him from going to prison, or waking up in the middle of the night bathed in cold sweat as the guilt of taking a human life haunted him. (Yes, if his Deadgirl wasn't a willing volunteer, he'd have to kill her after he fulfilled his fantasy. He didn't want to have to wear a mask or use a voice disguiser app. JT and Wheeler hadn't worn masks, right?)

Maybe he should let this go. He'd always have the movie, and his masturbation hand worked just fine.

Yet, what if he met somebody, got married, had kids, and the fantasy eluded him forever? Now was his chance, when he was still single and free of adult responsibilities.

What would the people who made *Deadgirl* think?

Stanley could pretty much guarantee they would not approve. If their movie implied that JT and his crew were in the wrong, they definitely would not be in favor of kidnapping and assaulting a real-life girl.

But if they didn't want him to do this, maybe they shouldn't have created such a compelling film.

He'd sleep on it. Decide in the morning.

* * *

When Stanley woke up the next morning and checked his phone, he'd received a notification that the *Deadgirl* novelization by Bridgett Nelson had shipped. It was a sign! He was definitely going to do this!

There wasn't an abandoned nuthouse near him, but there was a condemned hotel with a creepy basement. It had a metal table that would work just as well as the gurney in the movie. He could buy some chains from Home Depot without arousing suspicion. Stores were no longer selling Halloween supplies, and he didn't want to order anything online that might come back to bite him in the ass, but surely it would be easy to find some regular makeup that would make her look like Deadgirl.

Now he just needed a gun. That would be the hard part.

* * *

Or not.

As it turned out, the old guy at the pawn shop, who wore a shirt that had a picture of a gun and the phrase, "I Don't Call 911," was perfectly happy to sell him an extremely inexpensive pistol for "target practice." No ammo, but Stanley didn't need any bullets—the gun was purely for show. When it came time to kill Kylie, he'd strangle her.

* * *

He knew where she lived, of course. "My parents won't be home until 5:00," she'd assured him, as she took off her shirt, so he had that information as well. She walked home from school, so all he had to do was drive and get there a few minutes before her.

His car wouldn't be in her driveway for long. If a neighbor saw it, he'd say that, yes, he showed up to talk to her, but she blew him off for a hookup she'd arranged with some stranger she met online.

"What the fuck are you doing here?" Kylie asked, walking up her driveway. Stanley stood next to his car, his hand in his jacket pocket.

"I just want to talk."

"You're being scary. Get the fuck out of here before I call the cops."

Stanley pulled the pistol part of the way out of his pocket. "If you do, I'll kill you and then I'll kill myself. Get in my car. Right now. I only want to talk."

Kylie glanced at her front door, as if trying to decide if she could make it before he shot her.

"Be smart," he told her. "Don't scream. I have nothing to lose."

She got in the car.

* * *

"I'll give you another chance," she said, as they drove away. "It's just that I was developing feelings for you, and it scared me, so I pushed you away."

"Don't do that," Stanley told her. "Don't lie to me."

"Then what did you want to talk about?"

"I don't want to talk. Which I guess means that *I* lied to *you.* Ironic, huh? Anyway, enjoy the drive."

* * *

When they pulled up to the abandoned hotel, which looked as if a heavy rainfall could bring it crashing to the ground, Kylie seemed to realize that he hadn't brought her there for a conversation.

Ideally, this would've been the point where he injected her with a hypodermic needle or slapped a chloroform-soaked rag over her mouth. But, whereas, the gun had been easy, acquiring something to knock her out was a seemingly impossible task. So he forced her out of the car at gunpoint, then resorted to the primitive method of beating the shit out of her with a baseball bat.

A small part of him was proud and relieved that she hadn't kicked his ass instead. That had always been a possibility. But, no, there she was, lying on the ground, unconscious and bleeding.

A much larger part of him felt sick to his stomach. That hadn't been anywhere *near* as satisfying as he would've hoped.

Stanley dragged her inside the building and into the basement. He stripped her naked and got her onto the table, where he'd set up the chains the last time he was there. He applied the makeup, which ended up looking so different from the way Deadgirl looked in the movie, that he gave up and wiped it all off. Then he duct-taped her mouth, and...

...found himself completely lacking in horniness.

That was fine. That was perfectly fine. JT hadn't banged Deadgirl right after they found her. He could save that for a future visit.

He drove home, feeling nauseous with self-loathing.

There was a package waiting for him from Encyclopocalypse

Publications. He couldn't wait to read the book version of his favorite movie! That would help get his mind off what he'd done to Kylie.

He stayed up all night reading.

What the fuck was this?

It gave Deadgirl a backstory! Her fucking name was Ivy! The book tried to elicit sympathy for her—how the hell was he supposed to root for JT? The moral issue he had with the movie was way worse in the book. As far as Stanley was concerned, the author should be on that goddamn table, not Kylie!

He didn't even want to rape Kylie anymore. The book had ruined it.

* * *

The next day, various students were pulled out of class and questioned by the police about her disappearance. Stanley was truthful about his first visit—well, *mostly* truthful, leaving out his erectile dysfunction and replacing it with, "We realized we didn't have a condom." He decided to proceed as if there'd been no witnesses yesterday, using the "I wanted to get together again, but she'd made plans with some guy she met online," story he'd rehearsed. The part where he'd driven to her house was never mentioned.

The police seemed satisfied. He was definitely still a suspect, but there was no vibe that the walls were closing in.

That said, it didn't seem safe to return to the building where he'd left Kylie. Not yet.

That night, he went out to his backyard, tossed the *Deadgirl* book onto the grill, doused it with lighter fluid, then set that bullshit novelization on fire.

Then he tried to live his life normally.

The cops questioned him again the next day, to ask for more details about Kylie's online hookup. He apologized for having so little to offer them.

Three days after he left Kylie chained to the table, he wondered if she'd died from dehydration yet.

Five days after he left her, he was sure she was dead.

A week passed without the authorities breaking down his door. He felt sick whenever he saw a "Missing" poster of Kylie, and he saw those goddamn things everywhere.

A second week passed. Kylie wasn't found. If he'd been under surveillance, surely they'd have quit by now. They didn't have the resources to follow a single high school student 24/7.

He snuck out of the house in the middle of the night and drove to the abandoned hotel.

She was still in the basement.

She looked awful. Horrific. Smelled worse. There was no trace of the sexiness of Deadgirl. She was simply a rotting corpse.

It was disgusting.

But he hadn't gone through all of this not to fuck her.

The experience couldn't have been less satisfying.

Even though he tugged on her hair to jiggle her head and simulate feral consciousness, he could barely get hard enough to shove it in, and she was so dry inside, it hurt.

After the third thrust, he gave up.

It was awful. He'd probably never watch *Deadgirl* again. His favorite movie had been ruined for him, forever.

Tomorrow he'd begin the process of disposing of her body. For now, he just wanted to go home and cry.

As he walked toward the building's exit, he saw red and blue flashing lights through the window.

Wow. They had more resources than he thought.

Okay, so, should he surrender peacefully, or go out in a hail of gunfire?

He returned to the basement.

He was pretty much screwed no matter what, so he decided he might as well provide the cops with an image that would never leave their minds. He wouldn't be accomplishing anything else in life, so his legacy could be severe psychological damage.

He quickly stripped out of his clothes and mounted Kylie's corpse. He was completely limp, but he could at least give them the softcore experience. Hearing footsteps nearby, and somebody shouting through a megaphone, he began to thrust as hard as he could.

Hell, maybe they'd use this as the basis for *Deadgirl 2...*

AUTHOR'S NOTES

I first watched *Deadgirl* in late 2009 or early 2010. Back in those days, Netflix still sent actual DVDs in the mail. I'd study their list of horror movies intently, eventually making my choice. Impatient, I'd wait for it to arrive, run to the mailbox in excited anticipation, then set the red-and-white envelope on the TV stand and promptly forget about it for at least a month, sometimes more.

When *Deadgirl* showed up on their option list, I didn't have to think...I ordered it. A few days later, I watched it beginning to end. Obviously low-budget but really well done, the film stuck with me for a long time afterward. I couldn't get it out of my head.

The performances were top-notch, the storyline compelling. And yes, a few scenes were cringey as fuck. But it was the deadgirl herself, this long-abandoned young woman in the dungeon-like sub-basement of a mental health facility, that crept into my brain and took up real estate. For years.

Who was she? How did she get there? What was her story?

I eventually ordered the DVD for my home library and watched it a few more times.

You see, *Deadgirl* was never a zombie to me. Sure, she was

feral. Wild. Even animal-like. But she was also a person. And, like all of us, she deserved to have her story told.

Since 2008, when this movie debuted on the film festival circuit, the world has changed…especially for women. From the #MeToo movement, to the Pussyhat Project, to the Speak Out Act, to the overturning of Roe vs. Wade. Indeed, on January 26, 2025, as I write this (listening to the NFL playoff games in the background), our federal government has decided they have the right to make decisions about my uterus.

Wish I was joking.

My daughter is twenty years old, and she's coming of age in an era when all the forward momentum for women's rights, all the progress we've made in the past sixty years, has come to a sickening, screeching halt.

It's another reason I wanted to give *Deadgirl*, or, as I like to call her, *Ivy*…an identity. Because she's so much more than a slab of meat on a cold table.

More than a receptacle.

More than a punching bag.

And far more than a vessel.

She *was* a woman who was silenced.

I've given her a voice.

Bridgett Nelson
February 2025

ABOUT THE AUTHOR

Once an operating room registered nurse, Bridgett Nelson so enjoyed playing with human organs, she decided to turn her macabre interest into a horror writing career. She loves bubble baths (because nothing says spooooky writer like orange-scented bubbles), hates not knowing what's swimming in the water with her, lives for Halloween season (but loathes chainsaw-wielding dudes in haunted houses), adores her West Virginia University Mountaineers, is very pro-Oxford comma, and thinks bananas are absolutely disgusting.

Her first collection, *A Bouquet of Viscera*, is a two-time Splatterpunk Award winner, recognized both for the collection itself and its standout story, "Jinx." She is also the author of *Embracing the Profane, Poisoned Pink, What the Fuck Was That?, Sweet, Sour, & Spicy*, and her first novella, *Red Inside*, is now available!

Her work has appeared in multiple anthologies, and she was recently featured in the legendary Splatterpunk Zine.

Bridgett is working on her first original novel and a collaboration with a very funny writer.

Bridgett is mom to Parker and Autumn and a 2022 Michael Knost WINGS award nominee. She also won second-place in the '22 Gross-Out contest at KillerCon in Austin, Texas, and third-place in the '23 Gross-Out contest.

She currently lives in Duluth, Minnesota, with Bram Stoker Award-winning author, Jeff Strand, and their ball python, Indie Hellspawn McFangy Serenity Strand.